Praise for *The Book of Disbelieving*

"*The Book of Disbelieving* is filled with beauteous, beguiling wonders—giants of the deep, towers that stretch to infinity—but the most affecting magic here is profoundly human: the unknowability of others (and of ourselves); the mysteries of love and loss. Morse conjures the fantastic with such gorgeous, vivid precision we yearn for it to be real, much as his characters yearn to believe in each other."

—Peter Ho Davies, author of the Man Booker Prize-longlisted book
The Welsh Girl

"With its light touch, *The Book of Disbelieving* skillfully tracks how a change in worldview—subtle or bold—recreates the ways we look at society and one another. There's wild imagination here in the service of investigating relationships of all kinds—and each story reverberates beautifully into the next."

—Aimee Bender, author of *The Butterfly Lampshade*

"The stories in David Lawrence Morse's *The Book of Disbelieving* are located somewhere between what used to be called 'the real world' and the world of fables, mirror-realities, and dreams. This book carefully and patiently takes you into Wonderland, where nothing is quite what it seems. Reader, be prepared for a mind-bending journey to places you have never been before."

—Charles Baxter, author of *The Sun Collective*

"Set amid dreamscapes and dystopic worlds sometimes only at a slight angle to our own, David Lawrence Morse's *The Book of Disbelieving* explores grief, wonder, courage, (dis)belief, and the obligations we have to ourselves, our communities, and beyond. These stunningly inventive stories are filled with fascinating characters who confront the responsibilities of knowledge and change, mythos and desire, power and social order, and the day-to-day commitments of just moving through their worlds. Charming and mysterious, unsettling and moving, and always deeply alive, *The Book of Disbelieving* is an inspired collection of unique depth."

—Natalie Bakopoulos, author of *Scorpionfish*

"In the shiver-inducing tradition of Italo Calvino, Jorge Luis Borges, Shirley Jackson, and Margaret Atwood, David Lawrence Morse paints a vivid portrait of life in a universe eerily similar to our own. Intellectually provocative yet also deeply moving, these exquisitely written stories remind us of the comfort to be found in ritual and convention, along with the terror and joy to be found in freedom."

—Eileen Pollack, author of *Breaking and Entering*

"This is an astonishing debut. David Lawrence Morse has crafted nine short stories that share a wild inventiveness and sparkling ingenuity that will make believers of all who read *The Book of Disbelieving*. From 'Conceived,' the first of his fictions, to 'The Serial Endpointing of Daniel Wheal,' we're in the presence of a writer who's that rare thing: original. As another of his titles suggests, he will be 'Still With Us' in time and times to come."

—Nicholas Delbanco, author of *It Is Enough*

"What a marvel *The Book of Disbelieving* is! Here are cities filled with midwives and ferrymen for the dead, finishing schools for wife-auctions, and mysterious, prophetic journals of the recently deceased. It is a collection of love, of parenthood, and of our collective fears and dreams, set in worlds where the outskirts of cities still hold memories of unicorns and minotaurs, and families lash their homes to the backs of enormous whales. A brilliant and fabulous book of magical tales."

—Alexander Weinstein, author of *Children of the New World*

"The 21st-century fables in David Lawrence Morse's exquisite collection, *The Book of Disbelieving*, are finely wrought timepieces that contain within their works much strangeness and mystery. Each one lingers in the mind like a dream you can't quite shake after waking."

—Donovan Hohn, author of *The Inner Coast*

"In these riveting fables, Morse writes with lyrical beauty and biting humor to explore the precarious existence of individuals in societies driven by convention and delusion. Morse's extraordinary feats of imagination illuminate predicaments close to home: you will find yourself thinking about these stories for years to come."

—Edward Dusinberre, author of *Distant Melodies: Music in Search of Home*

THE BOOK OF DISBELIEVING

THE
BOOK OF
DISBELIEVING

David Lawrence Morse

SARABANDE BOOKS *Louisville, KY*

Publisher's Cataloging-in-Publication Data
(Provided by Cassidy Cataloguing Services, Inc.).

Names: Morse, David Lawrence, author.
Title: The book of disbelieving / David Lawrence Morse.
Description: Louisville, KY : Sarabande Books, 2023
Identifiers: ISBN: 978-1-956046-19-9 (paperback)
978-1-956046-20-5 (e-book)
Subjects: LCSH: Faith—Fiction. | God—Fiction. | Nature—Fiction.
Memory—Fiction. | Villages—Fiction. | Holidays—Fiction.
Widows—Fiction. | LCGFT: Fables. | Short stories. | Fantasy fiction.
Classification: LCC: PS3613.O778547 B66 2023 | DDC:
813/.6—dc23

Cover art is *Ahab's Sister* (2012) by Deedee Cheriel.
Cover design by Danika Isdahl.
Interior design by Alban Fischer.
Printed in USA.
This book is printed on acid-free paper.
Sarabande Books is a nonprofit literary organization.

This project is supported in part by an award from the National
Endowment for the Arts. The Kentucky Arts Council, the state arts
agency, supports Sarabande Books with state tax dollars and federal
funding from the National Endowment for the Arts.

For Jack and Phyllis Morse—who believed

CONTENTS

INTRODUCTION

The Book of Disbelieving is an apt title for this collection of stories that live in the fabulist realm.

An occurrence which defies expectation, usually against the logic of nature, is the shovel into the world of the fabulous and the surreal. This is the surprise at the heart of David Lawrence Morse's stories, which often have the flavor of a fable, or the eerie feeling of a nightmare. As in all fables and nightmares, death and violence loom, and yet in the hands of this writer there is a lightness and a sparkle in them, lifting them into a unique place.

In a time when the horizon was believed to be the edge of the world ("Death of the Oarsman") a man has power by knowing the truth. And still it reads like a fairy tale. The hilarious "The Great Fish" about people living on a fish, made me think of Donald Barthelme's "The Balloon" and playfully ups the ante to explore women's freedom.

David Lawrence Morse takes feathers from the caps of some of the great fabulists—Jorge Luis Borges, Italo Calvino and Gabriel García Márquez all peek from behind the curtain—and adds his own sly humor.

"Spring Leapers," about a town's yearly ritual, which begins comically and ends tragically, unfurls in the shadow of

Shirley Jackson's "The Lottery." (Can any surreal stories about a town's annual ritual escape the shadow of "The Lottery"?) This is also true of "The Market," where an annual auction showcases the age-old dynamic of women as commerce, and in this iteration is experienced from the point of view of a contemporary teenage girl.

David Lawrence Morse is a writer of imagination and whimsy. Some stories ask, What if? What if we all lived in a tower? What if a pregnant woman carried a child who refused to be born?

I was entertained by the soaring flights of fancy in many of these stories, but especially appreciated the more unique and less obvious ones. The success and elegance of "The Watch" lie in the writer's ability to allow a subtle surreal element to creep into the everyday, exploring the very real concerns of a marriage's dynamics, and of the struggle of a daughter's grief. It is quietly stunning. The showstopping title story, told in a deadpan matter-of-factness about a doorman's widowhood and discovery of a secret book, becomes an exploration into a number of things: the subjectivity of experience, the power of the imagination, and the tricks played by memory. Here the inane and the miraculous sidle up next to one another with a narrative voice bewitching and probing. David Lawrence Morse may have learned a thing or two in inspiration from the masters, but here he grows his own feathers and puts them in his own unique cap.

—SUSAN MINOT

So, as I too was vain enough to want to leave something to posterity, and didn't want to be the only one denied the right to flights of fancy, and since I had nothing truthful to report (not having experienced anything worth recording), I turned to lying. But I am much more honest in this than others: at least in one respect I shall be truthful, in admitting that I am lying. Thus I think that by freely admitting that nothing I say is true, I can avoid being accused of it by other people. So, I am writing about things I neither saw nor experienced nor heard about from others, which moreover don't exist, and in any case could not exist. My readers must therefore entirely disbelieve them.

—LUCIAN OF SAMOSATA, *A True History*

THE GREAT FISH

Our village is built atop the great fish, Ceta, a creature so capacious we have room for nineteen huts, lashed to her back with belts of kelp. Our huts are grouped in two rows, facing each other across the bony length of Ceta's spine from her dorsal fin to blowhole. My hut is closest to the blowhole, so I can monitor it, keep it free of debris—fish lice like to force their way into those warm, wet recesses. And even a small child, crawling loose and free, is liable to fall in, become wedged in the delicate tracheal membranes, suffocating our gentle Ceta. Who knows what she would do in such a situation? Thrash and flail the sea, flinging our meager posts and provisions miles across the deep? Perhaps, but Ceta is the gentlest of beasts, and also the wisest—she would see the futility in such aggression, knowing with a beast's instinctual wisdom that there's no cure for calamity once it has lodged itself inside. No, I imagine her simply sinking calmly into the sea, giving her flukes one last flip as if in apology, or farewell. Either way that would be the end of us.

It is my duty to see that Ceta has everything she needs. I swim into her mouth daily, clutching the great bony beak of a swordfish, with which to pick her baleen clean—the bigger fish sometimes get stuck between those hard, horny plates, causing her some discomfort. It's not easy work, finding my way in that great black chasm, swimming through the krill, but Ceta is patient and tries to keep her gullet shut so I won't get swallowed up inside. Sometimes these days I think of giving in to the temptation, of releasing my grip on the baleen, letting my body be taken up in that violent stream, swallowed along with millions of krill for the sake of a larger life. But that would mean abandoning my duty, and I assume Ceta's stomach would have no room for the likes of me—I'm a stubborn man and probably not easily digested.

Other villagers take care of the remaining matters—harvesting the fish lice, our primary source of food, also a danger to Ceta if too many accumulate too quickly. Lice attach themselves to her skin, trying to suck the very life out of her. But if you know how to grip them—just above the gut—they pluck right off, and make for easy eating—succulent, nothing but muscle, tasty raw or pickled in vats of brine. And our drinking water must be collected—every few minutes Ceta spouts forth a mighty mist, the water always remarkably warm, no matter the temperature of the sea, and free of salt.

Osa loved Ceta almost as much as I did, but was afraid she might suddenly make a dive for the deep, giving up her commitment to a surface existence. But Osa had many such fears. I never knew anyone who regarded the simple things of life with such simultaneous passion and suspicion. She was afraid of drowning, though she loved to swim. Afraid of swallowing her own teeth (they might make a meal of her from the inside out), though she loved to eat. Her greatest fear was of being misunderstood, though the life she lived was a mystery. But not a mystery to me, or at least I thought as much at the time. Understood? What is there to understand? We live on a fish on the sea. We eat fish lice and occasionally a lungfish, a tench, or a snook. We play with our children and make love with our wives. Life is good, life is not so good. We are glad, we are not so glad. What is there, I would ask my Osa, to understand?

I call her my Osa, though she was never properly mine—not my wife, anyway—only my companion. Companions are not allowed to marry unless and until they have produced a child—human life is too precarious to allow a couple to pass through life without propagation. If after a few seasons the companions have not succeeded, then they are separated and a new pair is arranged. I was Osa's second companion. Her first was set adrift on a raft of kelp after he was discovered to be impotent, which is not punishable in and of itself (we are not pitiless) except combined with his deceit—the couple had flaunted our customs regarding fertility in order to attend to their own notions of togetherness. Osa herself never confessed—it was her younger sister, Tama, who overheard them discussing it and told the elders. Osa was only spared the same sentence because as a probable childbearer she was entitled to another chance.

As for me, I was surprised to find Osa was interested at all. Her first companion, Conger, was one of the men who rode bareback on the dolphins, hunting with spears the larger game—swordfish, mako sharks—as much to protect our Ceta from attack as for fresh meat and hides. Osa would often ride the dolphins with them—not on the hunts but at other times, just for fun—and I would sit in envy, not of their prowess but of the wonderfully free way in which they rode. But some months after Conger had been exiled, Osa began to join me in the sea when I would inspect Ceta's sides for signs of illness or evidence of attacks. We would swim underneath her, admiring her massive dimensions, her jaws yawning open and her throat swelling to twice its size, swallowing the sea. Once we found a fresh wound on her belly—a gash of jagged flesh as long as my arm, the tooth of a mako shark lodged in the fat—which fascinated Osa so much I couldn't bring her to leave. Wounds, scars, scabs, blisters, sores—the evidence of injuries and how they healed—these captivated her. She was passionate about bodies and their processes, which was the reason she became obsessed with me: caretaker of the largest body in the sea.

Though ours was not her first companionship, I was surprised to find she approached it with the passion and ingenuousness as if it were. In our first weeks together, we were en route on our fish from the seas of summer to those of fall, the cool darkness of the deep, by degrees, seeping closer to the sea's surface. We moved together into one of the huts set aside for companions, and she brought with her many additions—variously colored sea stars to surround our pallet and a briny ball of orange, with brilliant, serpentine tendrils, to hang like the sun from our ceiling. The waters were still moderately warm at that time and we spent our days splashing and laughing and swimming with the others, the quicker swimmers among us catching tench for all to eat, the smaller children taking turns on the blowhole to be shot wriggling into the air, a few of us lying flat on Ceta's flukes to be flipped high into the sky, and my own Osa climbing onto the backs of the dolphins and holding on for the ride. At her goading the two of us dove down into the cold sea-deep, and there, unseen, lost in darkness, suspended together in the giant writhing silence, I first knew the reach and rush of lust.

And yet she didn't conceive, and soon our fish had brought us to winter seas, stretching before us calm and cold, Osa said, as a corpse. The sun far-flung, for months unmoving above, and I found my Osa gradually given to fits of ill humor. She hated the cold and monotony of those winter seas, where nothing much exists but ourselves and the occasional shadow of something silent in the deep, and her body began to show it. Her brown hair, a surge of curls and tresses, began to wilt, become long and sodden as seaweed. Her eyelids thickened; the soft corners of her mouth hardened with suspicion. In winter we rely almost entirely on the fish louse for food, but Osa lost her taste for these. And while others enjoyed the weather of these winters—the crisp, brisk touch of the sun—Osa was always chilled.

Her younger sister, Tama, didn't help matters. Tama frequently frustrated my efforts to care for Ceta, hiding the swordfish beak I used to clean the baleen, or worse, using the beak to pick at Ceta's skin, which I would then rub down for hours with shark fat. But when I mentioned this to Osa she refused to scold her sister and insisted that I leave her alone as well. "She's harmless," Osa said, "just a girl really. And can you blame her if she's bored?"

"Bored?" I asked. "How could one be bored? We're surrounded by the sea, the sky, the stars. Every day Ceta swims us somewhere different—the colors of the waters—see how they're changing!" But Osa's sympathies seemed to be more with her sister than with me, and we grew increasingly hostile. She was suspicious in her misery, sure that I disapproved, which was true, except I would not admit it, instead offering bitter sympathies. I could be caretaker, but only of something I thought deserved being cared for. What reason did Osa have for her petty ways?

"What reason?" she asked. "What reason does Ceta have for bringing us here?"

I told her Ceta didn't need a reason—any more than did the sun for sinking into the sea.

"Then I don't need a reason, either," she said. "Maybe one day I'll be riding a dolphin and decide to keep holding on, and never let go. Dolphins know where the warm waters are, and never leave them."

In such moments Osa would grow still, riveted by her own resentments, her cheeks reddening—in her anger she would forget to breathe. I was infatuated with her passions but angered when the passions pushed her the other way—from love of our life to hatred of it. She began to grant me little intimacy, though even at our most estranged I was fervent for it, from lust, but also from the growing realization that our time together would soon be ended by the elders unless our love proved fruitful.

The days were long in those winter waters and the nights nonexistent. Osa spent the time on our pallet, preoccupied with picking the calluses from her feet, or from mine, when I would let her. Or she would lie on the pallet resting on her elbows, studying the pallid gray patterns of Ceta's skin. When she did leave the hut, she would wander about looking for the sunburned boys—bribing them until they agreed to sit still while she peeled off their skin.

Our village spent much of these white nights in revelry, amid music of the drum and fife, spinning and slipping and dancing across Ceta's mottled skin, free from the sluggishness of sleep. I often observed these revelries—finding it enjoyable to watch others enjoying themselves—but Osa remained in our hut, determined to sleep. She didn't want to miss her dreams.

Sometimes she would describe these dreams to me, full of things none of us had ever seen: beings like fish that swam through the air rather than the sea; an expanse of surface, like our Ceta's back except vaster, firmer, more permanent; and from that surface, things growing upward, like seaweed but without need of water for support, fixed instead of floating, whispering in the breeze. She told me these were things she had dreamed into existence. She said that life inflicted wounds and that dreams were the mind's means of healing. She asked me if I ever dreamed and I—taken aback and even offended by her visions—lied for the first time and told

9

her I didn't. I told her dreams were the things of fools and prophets. She assumed I meant her to be a fool and left me alone on the pallet; I might have stopped her but I couldn't. In truth I didn't know which she was—fool or prophet—and didn't know if she knew, either.

Yet we maintained a fascination with each other—there were still flashes of passion. As once when we crawled onto our hut's roof, a shelf of kelp, to watch the winter lights—great green glowing bands dancing in the sky. *Swoot swoot BOOM* went the blowhole, and the spout shot high into those green sky lights, and we were awash in the heated mist, the seaweed soft and supple under our backs, and Osa asked me what did it all mean. I didn't know any more than she did, but I did know that wasn't what she wanted to hear, and for once I obliged her, and gave her meanings—fool that I was—as I understood them right then: that there was no such thing as time, only the glow of the moment; that there was no such thing as truth, only the blur of feeling and belief. She gasped and her eyes regained their wide, wild delight. "We shouldn't be up here," she said. "We could fall through." And then we fell to each other with such force that that is exactly what we did—fell through—the kelp suddenly letting us go so quickly and completely that it seemed impossible it had ever held us, and as we fell we remained embraced, suspended for a moment, blind in the green misty light, before we landed on the pallet, on Ceta's forgiving back, with an unforgiving thud.

"Where have you been?" she asked afterward. She was resting on my chest, her head rising and falling with my breaths.

"Where else? I've been right here."

"You mean with me?"

"Well, yes."

"You only love the idea of me. And I love the idea of you. But that's not enough."

"Wouldn't a child help with that?"

She was quiet for a while. Every few minutes the blowhole boomed. "No," she said. "A child would just be floating along with us. We wouldn't love our child, just the idea of our child."

"What's wrong with floating?" I asked. "That's the way the world works."

"But what if we weren't living on Ceta anymore? What if Ceta were free to swim and dive and leap out of the water like other fish, and we were free, too, without clinging to her back like lice. What if we found a place where what was under us wasn't always moving? *Then* I could settle down with you."

"What do you mean *then*?" I said. "There's no such thing as *then*. There's only now. Now is the same as it's always been. And always will be."

Again she was silent, then said bitterly, "I see." And I could feel the muscles in her back stiffening, feel them constricting. She rolled off my chest and away from me, and we lay there silently, separately, rising and falling with Ceta's tremendous breaths.

I can't remember which arrived first that spring—the rumors or the bird. The rumors said that the elders were already thinking of separating Osa and me; it was no secret, though

I'd tried to keep it so, that we were having difficulties. She now refused intimacy except on rare occasions, though at the same time, she refused to be finished with me. She thought she could somehow win me over to her dreams of things, and didn't believe me when I said I never dreamed. "You talk in your sleep," she said. "Sometimes you cry out—that's how I know you're lying." And it was true I was having dreams—but not like Osa's—her views had gotten under my skin, and I had secretly begun to fear what would happen to us if Ceta ever died. We had lived on her back for generations, so that we could no more imagine her dying than the sun itself, but then again, wasn't she a fish, just like the other fish of the sea? I began having nightmares, dreaming of an ocean of bones and foam and blood. I dreamed of Ceta sinking, and of the villagers lashed to her back, sinking through an abyss of krill. And yet my role as Ceta's caretaker was a sacred responsibility I could not easily disavow—as long as I continued to administer to her needs, then surely she would continue serving us dutifully as she had always done. And besides, I asked Osa, where were we to go? She was determined that I admit the possibility of her nightly visions, and I was determined that she admit the actuality of our situation.

I tried to seduce her while she slept, but she would wake, angry, and leave. She would go back to her father's hut. Sometimes when this happened Tama would make her way down Ceta's long bony spine, balancing, her arms outstretched like fins. She would sing to herself, "Osa's home, Osa's home," loud enough that the villagers in their huts on either side might hear. When she arrived at my hut she would stop in the doorway, a hand on the frame, looking at me, and announce, "Osa's home."

"Yes, I know."

"Do you know why?"

"Because she loves her little sister."

"Don't be a fool," she would say—reproving me, but reproving Osa, too, whose love could not be had or held so simply. And then she would make up a preposterous list of reasons why her sister had come home: Osa lost her eyes again—Papa is gluing on new ones. Osa forgot to kiss the great fish in the sky goodbye before she was born—she has to go back and be born again. Osa likes to sleep with Papa. Osa peeled off all her skin.

One day she didn't stop at the doorway but slipped inside, keeping her hands behind her. She started again on her list: Osa swallowed a fish louse whole. Osa exploded. Osa came home to find her sister but her sister turned into a bird.

"What's a bird?" I asked.

"Here," she said, and held out her cupped hands. Inside them was the strangest thing I'd ever seen, like something out of Osa's dreams. A snout like that of a swordfish, long and beaked, which opened and shut and emitted strange squeaks. A plump body, shaped more like a large fish egg than a fish itself, with a thin, wrinkled membrane of skin, and strange, soft fins that alternately extended and were tucked away.

"What is it?" I asked.

"A bird, silly," Tama said. "Osa created it, in one of her

dreams. But she's never seen a real one. I'm the only one who has. Me, and now you, too."

"Where did you get it?"

"It got me. It landed on my head. Here, you can hold it," she said, and reached toward me, but the bird sprang out of her hand and began swimming through the air, beating what I only knew then to call its fins. "That's okay," she said. "In Osa's dreams that's called flying." The bird flew out my cabin door but Tama remained unconcerned. "It'll come back," she said. "I'm its new home."

Only the bird didn't come back, but was seen by various villagers swimming—flying—in and out of huts, over heads and under arms, until it landed in the hands of Tope, one of the elders, a timid man with enormous eyes, who clutched at it and almost broke its neck before his wife got it into a makeshift cage. There was a commotion in the village such as had not been seen since years before, when an old woman named Daee declared our great fish pregnant, and it was only after many speeches from me that I convinced the village Ceta wasn't pregnant but was only suffering from indigestion. "How could she possibly conceive?" I told them at the time. "She's twice as big as any fish out there."

Everyone took the bird's arrival as a sign—but of what? Some thought it meant the end of times, which brought leaping and laughter from some, crying from others. Some quarreled, hitting each other in the knees with bones. Others played the fife and drum, marching up and down Ceta's spine. Others feasted, opening up the reserves of pickled plaice, or plucking off fresh fish lice and biting them in half. Games of gobo, shinny, and battledore, wrestling and fencing, spouting contests among the boys. Only, in the uproar, the villagers lost track of the bird itself, and when a line formed around Tope's hut, waiting to give him his ceremonial, congratulatory whacks on the back for a notable deed done, it was discovered that Tope himself no longer had the bird—he said it was at Turbot's. Turbot said it was at Tautog's. Tautog said it was at Sprat's. Sprat didn't know where it was, or even that it existed, Sprat having died the previous week. His widow beat the villagers out of her hut with a dead lungfish.

Late that night, Osa returned to the hut, as I knew she would. There was no moon and the night was black and the sea winds unusually strong for the season, and I felt as if I were lost and swirling inside the sea-filled jaws of a beast even greater than Ceta, without her bony baleen to hold on to, to keep me from giving myself to the rush of darkness swallowing us all. Osa paused in the doorway, I couldn't see her but could feel her presence, her eyes wide and fixed on where she knew my body would be lying. She feared doorways—that feeling of being caught in between—but she lingered there, as her sister had done so many times before.

"Would you believe me if I told you I conceived the bird in a dream?" she asked, her voice trembling, her words tumbling down onto me as if from a great height. I was staring into the night through the tattered hole in the roof, which she'd insisted I never repair, so that the mist from Ceta's breaths drizzled down upon us.

"No," I said.

"Would you believe me if I said the bird flew to us from a great expanse of something called land, and that we could live there, you and I?"

"No," I said.

"Would you believe me if I said I have conceived a child? Our child?"

My heart kicked at my breast, but though I wanted to believe her, again I said no. To believe one of her conceits was to believe them all, and to believe them all was to risk the ruination of the precarious life it was my responsibility to preserve.

"I see," she said, and was silent. Ceta's spouts boomed and the warm mist fell upon us, and I could feel Osa sinking away from me, sinking back into the night.

By noon the next day the entire village had been given to understand that Osa was with child—it was Tama who triumphantly spread the word. The village decided the mysterious bird must have been a messenger bringing the news, and there were whispers that Osa was to bear a child of great strength and courage. Most were pleased that the end of times was to be put off after all, though a few dissenters said the child might be the one who would one day wreak the ruin. All the men—including Osa's father—lined up to whack me on the back (some of the shark hunters hit harder than they should), and in the afternoon three elder women arrived with pillows and fragrances and a tiara of pike teeth for the mother-to-be. Only Osa had not yet returned to our hut from the night before, and I had not gone to find her. The women stumbled about in the hut, embarrassed and concerned and titillated, adjusting and readjusting the pillows on the pallet and chattering.

"It's a hardness on a woman, who's with child."

"A man's no help anyways."

"Could be a demon-child."

"No telling what a woman might do."

"Come to her good sense eventually."

The villagers were befuddled. Marriage festivities were in order yet couldn't proceed if the couple didn't seem inclined to be together. As for me, in the following days I busied myself in the sea with Ceta. Now that she'd returned us to warmer waters I had many duties: cleaning the yellow algae from beneath her flippers, rubbing down her flippers and dorsal fin with vats of shark fat, filing the barnacles off her flukes. Difficult duties, but worth doing, keeping me in the sea and out of my vacant, newly fragranced hut. As for Osa, I missed her terribly and strove to know if what she said was true—that she had conceived a child. And yet I remained tormented by my own suspicions. What of what she'd said did she herself believe? We were suffering, as we had all along, from two different kinds of obstinacy—Osa's driven by the fervency of dream and belief, mine more like a disease, trapped within the accumulated fat of habit, insulation against a fear of the mysterious, that would not let me yield, and would not let me go.

A week passed. One of the elders—Tope himself, who had found and lost the messenger bird—came to me, his enormous eyes drifting in his cavernous sockets, and questioned me tepidly about the nature of our disagreements, suggesting I do what I could to resolve them. Tama could be heard about the village, singing out "Osa's home" to whomever looked as if they might want to hear. But she did not come again to my doorway, instead solving everyone's problems by coming to the elder women late one afternoon, crying and claiming that Osa was not pregnant after all. Osa had neglected to throw away the strips of kelp she'd used to clean herself, and Tama had found these and was here bringing them to the elders. The elders made their decision swiftly, this being Osa's second offense against fertility, that she was to be put on a raft of kelp and set adrift at sea.

The entire village seemed in agreement, except her father, who tarried in the doorway when the shark hunters arrived to carry her away. But even he put up little fight—just a gatherer of fish lice his entire life. It was said Osa seemed willing to go. It was said she forgot to kiss our Ceta, the great fish, goodbye. It was said she took nothing with her. It was said that her raft didn't drift at all, but seemed moved by unseen currents, and that a bird flew overhead, leading, circling, following.

It was Tama who said these things, lingering, swinging in my doorway. It was Tama who told me proudly that it was her own blood that had bloodied the kelp, her first time, and just in time, for Osa really had conceived a child, but had placed her sister under oath not to tell.

"Why?" I asked, clutching at my throat, feeling my airway constricting. "Because she wanted to die?"

"Oh, don't be such a fool," she said.

Only now I have little choice but to be the fool, love-lost, fearful of what may become of us, lying on my back by night, showered by Ceta's mists, admiring and scrutinizing the nature of her spouts. Are they coming less frequently? Are they blowing at not quite their former height? Is our Ceta slowing down? I do not know, and cannot, nor can I know what became of my Osa alone out there on a raft of bones, but every day I keep watch on the horizon for that mysterious expanse of something called land, and imagine my Osa running and spinning and dancing across it, our child clinging to her back, laughing, holding on for the ride.

THE BOOK OF DISBELIEVING

When Paul Sorser's wife died she left him with a hodgepodge of books and clothes, some houseplants, the box of recipe cards on the shelf, the floppy disks from her project on cab-drivers begun long ago, and her collection of artifacts from her family's past. Paul was a custodian, a loyal employee for eighteen years, and they gave him a week of leave. He insisted on two and they said, with regrets, that one week was allotted by the union but he could take a second if he was willing to forgo pay. The management sent an arrangement to the service and after a week he returned to work.

He had few friends who were not Alice's friends, or husbands of Alice's friends, and in the weeks that followed her death he resisted their offers of commiseration. She had possessed such leisurely ferocity. She could transform boredom into the most pleasant idleness but though he had known what to do with leisure in her company, he did not know what to do with it now. He sought some way to keep busy and he found himself going through the boxes of her family's artifacts with the intention of passing them along to her relatives. There were newspaper clippings of her great-grandfather's breakthroughs in agriculture; there were the ribbons and medals earned by more than one ancestor in more than one war; there were diplomas from universities and napkins on which were scribbled the geneses of profound ideas; there were photographs and sketches and portraits and eulogies; there were newsletters providing updates on the Thorntons' whereabouts and accomplishments; there was a knife carved from soapstone as fine and light as a feather and a scroll seventeen feet long—but the only thing Paul wanted to keep was the sword from the War. He couldn't remember to which relative it had belonged nor its political significance (though the story had been told many times) and he didn't care. The sword seemed out of place in the city and now, without his wife, he felt out of place, too. His character was not suited to the city and without her fondness for its ways or skill overcoming its inconveniences he felt robbed of purpose and usefulness. He knew how to work with his hands. Outside the city he might apprentice himself to a furniture maker or some other craftsman but he was past fifty and the country was vast and to leave this apartment would be to expose himself to unknown risks. He kept the sword and sent the rest to his wife's aunt Jude.

Three weeks later he received a package from Aunt Jude with a note—*Thank you but I cannot keep this, fascinating as it may be.* It was a book with a stiff cardboard cover, bound in brown-check cloth, of large, square bulk with an attached ribbon bookmark; he must have assumed it was another scrapbook. But there were no pictures or clippings, just the uninterrupted flow in ink of his wife's small hand. Each entry was dated and of the same approximate length. How had his wife managed to keep such a meticulous journal without his knowledge? She was secretive, but she maintained secrets only on matters of little importance. It had been almost a decade before he'd discovered that she hated the color red. Only recently had she revealed that she kept her hair long out of homage to a certain folk singer. These secrets, she admitted, she harbored not to sow discord between them but to protect some part of herself from inquiry. On momentous matters she was always frank: she'd confessed her affair the day after it was begun and made no secret of her aversion to his mother. So this journal, he concluded, must be of little consequence—a memento of those quiet, private moments one finds like small marvels hidden in the day. He expected to read about a luna moth clinging to the window screen or the Easter lily's fragrant blooms or the kind words she heard at work. He started to read somewhere at random and was startled to discover that the journal was about him.

He doesn't know if the problem is with the regulator or the siphon so he sketches the valve and takes the sketch to Harbin's who suggests tempering the regulator and he tries it and it works. Sam Borger tips him thirty even though he saved Sam a trip from the plumber and one-fifty at least. But it's the biggest tip Paul's gotten since he put out the fire on the Draytons' grill. He bought two Polish dogs with extra kraut and ate them on the Wideners' terrace. They've been out of town since Monday.

This was an entry from almost fifteen years ago. He had no memory of the incident but it all sounded plausible—except for the part about the Wideners' private terrace. He didn't believe he was the kind of fellow who would do something like that. And he didn't reveal details like these to his wife—not because, like her, he wanted to keep a part of his life secret but because none of it was worth remembering. Where the heck did she learn about tempering regulators? *The Hogans' son-in-law—Paul couldn't remember his name—was taking away some of the furniture and put too much on the cart and when he got the cart on the sidewalk the meter maid arrived to write him a ticket. He didn't get a ticket but left to move the van, leaving Paul to wheel the cart back into the lobby and the glass dome on a pendulum clock fell off and shattered. Marilyn Cantwell arrived with her spaniel and complained about the glass and Paul got in trouble with the super. The son-in-law isn't a bad fellow but he only comes twice a year, he's cheap, which Paul doesn't mind, but he's in a hurry, which Paul minds very much.* That was an entry from near the end of the volume, nine years ago. Paul remembered the son-in-law very well, though he couldn't remember his name or an incident with a cart of furniture.

He closed the book, put it down. He was not easily agitated, but the book unnerved him. Had she found some way to watch him? To monitor him at work and record his activity in her book? It was a feat that verged on the supernatural and he couldn't escape the feeling that if she had found some way to watch him then, she might also be watching him now. Paul didn't believe in spirits just as he didn't believe in unicorns or minotaurs or other myths from a superstitious age. He preferred to think that his wife was at work when she was at work and that she was buried in the ground when she was buried in the ground. It was only early afternoon but he opened a beer. He stood at the window watching the punks on the corners five stories below and the children gathering trash and throwing it down a grate and the vendor with his boxes of T-shirts and unsavory fruit and the occasional pedestrian passing by without interest. The vendor was equally uninterested in his wares. He slouched against a newspaper rack and shouted trifles at an old man in a window and his bitter grin revealed his wish to be elsewhere. Paul wrapped the book in the newspaper in which it had been shipped and returned it to Aunt Jude's box and placed it carefully under the bed. He was not a sentimental person. He didn't talk to the image of his dead wife or imagine what she would be thinking or indulge in reminiscences or thumb through old photographs or revisit old haunts. It didn't occur to him to remember the past or think what might have been had a doctor discovered in time the weakness in her heart. On days when he felt lonely, he attributed it to lack of sleep or frustration with the management or the rudeness of a tenant. He went for long, slow walks with his hands in his pockets as he had always done and he marveled at the self-importance and ingenuity of city people as he had always done. Since reading the excerpts from his wife's journal he was having trouble getting her out of his mind, and his work and tenants seemed alien to him, as if in need of the interpretation his wife offered in the book.

For an entire evening he eschewed gin or beer to devote himself to the task of remembering and finally came up with the memory that he required. Out from under the bed he pulled the book and unwrapped the newspaper carefully as if he were removing the bandages from a wound. There were hundreds of pages and they were fine like the leaves of a Bible and the date of each entry was hard to discern. Finally he found it—their tenth anniversary. On that day, he remembered, the Finnicums on the fourth floor asked him to come up to investigate a rat but when he arrived with a box of poison and some no. 2 steel wool they surprised him with an anniversary card and a slice of homemade pie. He read Alice's entry for that day but found no mention of the incident, only a description of the activities of a team of restoration specialists called in to remediate a burst pipe. Did this prove that his wife's account was fictional? The incident she described on that day sounded convincing. It might have occurred in addition to the anniversary card from the Finnicums.

Again he wrapped the book in newspaper and put it away. The next day he called Aunt Jude. But once she came on the line (this took some time as Uncle William had to retrieve her from the sewing machine in the basement), Paul couldn't figure what to say without revealing his suspicion that either his wife or his wife's aunt was deceiving him. Aunt Jude asked after his health and suggested a program at the zoo for widowers that she'd read about in the paper. He asked Jude if she had any interest in a book he'd just found under a stack of cookbooks, full of old family recipes that his wife seemed to have copied by hand. Yes indeed, Jude said, what an absolutely marvelous find—she was certainly interested.

And she informed him what a wonderful person his wife was for taking such care in preserving her family's memories. "But I don't need to tell *you* about the importance of memories," said Jude. "I know you won't mind but I did read a few pages of your journal, I couldn't help myself. I never could have imagined that the chores of a custodian would be so interesting! And how kind of Alice to transcribe it for you. Her penmanship was exquisite and yours is dreadful."

Who writes a book about someone other than themselves? Alice had not been a selfless person. She was not one of these wives devoted to her husband's every need. She was devoted to the needs of her clients from nine to five. Otherwise in her spare time she worked hard at making sure she was not stressed by trivial concerns nor those of her husband. He had no resentments on this score. But why the devil had she composed this chronicle of the dreary business of his life? And why had she stopped the journal a decade ago after dedicating herself to it for so long? If he remembered correctly, that might have been the time that she started experimenting with various hobbies although nothing stuck. Pottery, tap dancing—even mime. Why had she given them up? He wasn't sure, but he thought it had to do with new responsibilities at work. It was possible there were other volumes of the journal but he searched every closet and found none. He called her sister but her sister said she knew nothing of Alice's writing and instead lamented at length her abrupt death.

He didn't look at the journal for a week then pulled it out

from under the bed and unwrapped the newspaper and began to read starting on the first page and he kept reading through the night and into the next day and beyond the time he was meant to man the door for work and all the day, ignoring the phone calls from the super and reading one entry after another, all the entries, which were written in the same careful, unrushed hand, with the same pen, it seemed, which apparently never ran out of ink. It was as if the book had been composed in a single sitting and he read it in a single sitting: how, in his early days, like the tenants with dogs, he was only allowed to take the service rather than the glossy elevator with its brass and mahogany; how the bags of trash split on impact at the bottom of the chute and how he drove away rats with a stick; how he polished the brass rails with Frausto's Spangled Cream, which smelled like bacon grease and made the skin under his nails burn; how a tenant left an old pinball machine in the basement and he fixed the plunger and flippers but the super got rid of it for more storage; how he retreated into the old icebox for cigarette breaks until he gave in to management complaints and quit smoking at work; how the realtors didn't bother to introduce themselves and how certain solicitors would contrive to sneak in through the basement and, if caught, would try to foist onto Paul their cards; how it was possible, staring at the surveillance monitor for hours, to imagine hiccups in the rhythm of infinity; how the sound of the door buzzer made him feel as if he were the subject of some mean experiment; how he concocted pranks to play on the tenants, such as putting racy lingerie into the wash of the philandering family men, none of which he enacted; how he once slept an hour slumped at his station and though no one complained he woke with a note in his fist that read: *You owe me.*

He didn't remember any of it. Did they force him as the janitor to ride the service? Reading his wife's book made it sound so natural and accurate, it seemed the kind of thing the management would do but they didn't make the janitor do that now. It was all so long ago. The door opener *did* sound like the punishing buzz from some psychology lab but he didn't recall making this comparison before. He didn't remember any particular conflicts with realtors but it was true, now that he thought about it, that they were a snooty bunch and never introduced themselves unless they wanted something. But didn't that tall realtor with the gray demeanor, the one with the strange name, didn't he gift Paul a bottle of scotch? As custodian he had occasionally filled in as doorman but he did not recall staring at the surveillance monitor and he had no idea what his wife meant by the rhythms of infinity. He did not recall working on a pinball machine but even if he did, and the management made him get rid of it, that wasn't so unreasonable, was it? Space was at a premium and he was never good at those games anyway—he lacked quick reflexes and couldn't motivate himself to care about the accumulation of points.

He began to wonder whether his wife understood anything about him. How great was the gap between her version of his work and the work itself? He didn't know whether to marvel at her imagination or fret at her mendacity. Or was the book not fiction at all but an accurate rendering of his life—had his wife somehow managed to discover the intimacies of his labor like some kind of clairvoyant of the proletariat? She rendered in subtle terms his triumphs and humiliations at the hands of tenants and the management, and in her depiction of him as a working man she saw a figure clever and steadfast and seditious and shrewd. But the man she depicted was not the man she married and it occurred to him that perhaps she had written the book to inspire herself in the business of living. Other writers chose secret agents or accomplished generals or tycoons for their subjects but she had chosen him. It seemed a choice laden with significance, a choice, like her decision to marry him, that singled him out as some kind of exemplar and he was overcome by gratitude and doubt.

When he dropped in on management at the end of his second unexplained day of absence, the super explained that they understood this was a difficult time. He agreed to allow Paul to come back to work without saying another thing about it, but Paul wouldn't be paid for the two absent days. The super had downy tufts of hair atop both ears and a dab of mustache as light as froth. He wasn't the kind of man to come down hard on a fellow but he wouldn't tolerate disregard for responsibility and he looked on Paul with a humble expression of prerogative and held out his open hands and said, "Well?"

Paul didn't think he deserved to lose two days' pay, but

he didn't deserve to lose his job, either, and the prospect of unemployment made him shudder. To quit the job would be to honor Alice's nature rather than his own. His life was duller than she had imagined. He was nothing more than one of the fugitive figures passing across the monitor's screen. That night he cut a brown paper bag and wrapped the cover of his wife's book as he had schoolbooks as a child, and he thought of a title for the book and inscribed it on the front. The next morning he placed *The Book of Disbelieving* in the return bin at the branch library and resumed his position at the front door of the Concordian.

SPRING LEAPERS

The village of Hiram, thirteen miles southwest of Iamonia, the county seat, forty miles to the far edge of the wiregrass, the Omanockee River flowing like a thick ribbon of mud, and the villagers astir in their cabins, busy about their yards, already climbing onto their roofs—for it is the first Sunday of spring, and it is Leaping Day. Newlyweds Octie Bogue and his wife, Magaline, will leap clasped together, hoping if one is obliged, the other will be, too. After all, how could they find a mate in heaven better than the mate they've already got? Magaline can't help but find Octie endearing, with his ribald oaths of love, his quick and cataclysmic orgasms, his ropes and belts and buckles with which he will bind them breast to breast to take their leap.

"I love you like a house on fire," says Octie. "I love you like a bleeding wound."

"I love you, too, Octie Bogue," says Magaline.

Octie has acquired from the blacksmith a harness, fashioned according to special instructions, a double-wide wrought iron seat like a flat banana that they both straddle, facing each other, with ropes around the waist and over each shoulder. They stand together on the roof of their one-room broadaxe log cabin, making preparations for their leap, strapped into the harness.

"Not like that," says Octie.

"This is uncomfortable," says Magaline.

"Bend your legs," says Octie.

"Can't we just hold hands?" asks Magaline.

Octie makes some adjustments to the ropes around his waist and hers.

"Put your legs over mine. I'll hold up the both of us," says Octie.

"No," says Magaline.

"Why not?" says Octie.

"Because it's lewd and vulgar," says Magaline.

"Damn right," says Octie, pawing at her legs.

"Stop it," says Magaline.

"Come on, let's put the devil in hell."

"Not on Leaping Day," says Magaline.

"Why not?" says Octie.

"Because it's lewd and vulgar," says Magaline.

Octie has managed to pull one of her legs up over his but she withdraws her leg and withdraws herself from the harness. Octie experiments with the harness for a few minutes. "All right," he says. "We'll sit the other way, like a horse." They try sitting the other way, like a horse, first with Magaline in front, then Octie. "There," says Octie.

"This is embarrassing," says Magaline.

———

Beulah Duckett no longer leaps on Leaping Day but this is not true of her husband Esco, who has broken his ankles or a wrist or leg every year leaping for the last eight years but still plans on leaping this morning, he has already bathed in the bucket tub and donned his striped wool suit, with the unhemmed trousers and rumpled billycock hat and plantation tie askew.

"What are you so awful bothered to leave us for?" asks Beulah, referring to herself and three kids, who are not yet old enough to leap and are frightened by their father's falls. Esco has just invited inside the Reverend Colonel, making the customary rounds on Leaping Day, and he nods to the Reverend and says to Beulah, "Haven't you ever in your life had the desire to take on a life with God?"

"What's God want with those old broken bones of yours?"

"Curses on your tombstone heart," says Esco. "Great God pardon the day I wed that tombstone heart."

God *might* pardon the heart, the Reverend Colonel explains to them, or he might not, it is not his place to say, all he can offer is his usual meager blessing, a waggle of his staff and sprinkle of dust, and—if they seem in need of inspiration for leaping—a short parable. *And lo, two soldiers took a long walk in a great field. And they came to a village, and one soldier said, "Shall we stop here?" And the other soldier replied, "No, we shall keep going."* The Reverend Colonel waggles his staff to indicate he is finished and Esco says how he loves a good parable, and Beulah asks what the devil does it mean. But the Reverend Colonel does not respond, only hobbles on his way, over the village's grassy paths and cobblestones with his wooden leg—the original was lost to a cannonball in the War—which he claims prevents him from leaping on Leaping Day, and the village grudgingly agrees. History has shown reverends are no good at the business. Most every right reverend left the village after only two or three years, unable to bear the scrutiny, the rumors, the criticism, their faith and authority each year on Leaping Day subject to proof. And the villagers were glad to see them go: If their own reverend was not called to God, then what hope for the rest? Prior to the Reverend Colonel there was the Reverend Whidden, who tried to excuse himself from any more leaps by protesting that his work was on earth, God's got no use for a reverend in heaven, but Wiley Cooper scoffed, "Somebody better notify Jesus—I think he's still up there." The Reverend Whidden left town soon after, his spine permanently awry from three years of collisions with the earth. Only one reverend had ever been obliged by God, but that was years ago, and some claimed he was never sighted rising to heaven but most likely beat a hot escape through Lost Hollow when no one was looking. Others like Old Aunt Myra doubted whether anyone was ever obliged; like a few other deep-timber seclusionists, she never took to leaping. "Well, now, I know there's a God somewhere," Aunt Myra liked to say, "because men couldn't do this business of living alone. But I'll never believe they go flying up there off the roof. God didn't intend that at all. A man will tell a story about anything, but is it true?" You can tame everything but the tongue, said the villagers of Hiram, and they brought her pig feet and corn pone, and they told her about the most recent villagers obliged. Sometimes it was the thriftiest villager, or the most pious, this was no surprise, but then there were the anomalies, like Darlie Sewell, the village tart, wearing those button shoes and gingham dresses, a widow, and kissing Monroe Gibbs at the candy pulls, and she obliged only last year. The villagers each leapt their own way, but all laughed if caught in the hand of God, rising into the white skies, obliged. Ticklish, ridiculous laughter, and the villagers on the ground standing mouths agape, averting their eyes from the sun, remnants on the earth.

The earth was hard-packed red clay in places, sandy topsoil in others, from which flourished the rampant tawny wiregrass and an unusually piquant variety of onion that enjoyed widespread regional popularity, irritating Lawton Dickey, the village literate, who never ate them and complained the air was permeated with the taste. For the villagers Lawton reads the odd piece of mail and writes epistles, as well as modest, epigrammatic epitaphs for those who die before being obliged. He carries a coin purse full of candy mints and sucks on one at all times, now he sucks on two, one he rolls on his tongue and the other he holds in reserve in the pouch between cheek and teeth. He is nervous, he must make a fateful decision: Will he leap off the tower or no? He stands at his window looking up at the tower, which carries about it an air of disintegration, an air of terror, hugging close to the ramshackle church to which it has been haphazardly attached, looming over the benign river village like the forlorn rampart of some forgotten castle along the Rhine. Lawton's father had the tower built twenty years ago. He'd intended it to be freestanding in the village green, a height closer to heaven from which to leap, but the reverend had suggested the project might find favor from the Lord if the tower was built attached to the church, and so it was, though Lawton's father found no favor when he leapt from it and fell to his death. No one had leapt from the tower since. Few sons are like their fathers, the villagers would say, most are worse, and this was true of Lawton Dickey, who was not the leaper his father was: when he leapt from his roof each spring, he landed in a heap and cried out in pain. He limped for days afterward, though no bone was broken, joking how God had forsaken him, but that was all right it happened to the best of them, even Jesus.

"What do you mean, Jesus?" his sister said.

"On the cross," Lawton said. "They nailed him up and whipped him with hot lashes."

"Jesus was the first leaper," she said. "Jesus leapt to heaven on the wings of the dove."

Lawton lives with his sister, who doesn't appreciate jokes about Jesus, or about leaping, or their father, synonymous with the sanctity of the everlasting God. The village has corrupted the practice of leaping, stumbling drunk off their rooftops and falling helplessly like half-wits onto bales of hay. "Leaping's not meant to be fun," she would say. "It's how to prove your faith." She has trouble with the rheumatism and so she keeps her skin oiled with pine oil, looking to Lawton malignant and content and greased as a spit pig. On this morning she is preparing everything for Lawton's big leap: already she's beaten the soles of his shoes with a persimmon stick, boiled the snakeroot tea, pressed their father's overalls with a hot stone. Lawton watches her.

"If you're all fired up to leap," he says, "you go throw yourself off that tower like a damn fool."

"You're calling our father a fool?"

Lawton rolls the candy mints over his tongue, watching the tower from the window. "First time was courageous," he says. "Second time's foolish."

"Someone's got to set an example for these idiots," says Lawton's sister.

"Then do it yourself," says Lawton.

"No one pays any attention to a woman," she says.

The village of Hiram is alive with leapers. Some emit involuntary yelps. Some stumble. Some throw their arms and legs wide. Some do backflips. Some require a push. Some are solemn. Some leap again and again. Most fall onto the hard-packed red-clay earth below, but then there is a shout of joy and there is Narcissa Moon lifted for all to see, laughing ticklishly, she blows kisses at some boy but no one is sure who, could be Roland Crisp, possibly Jule Shellnut, who takes inspiration from Narcissa's leap and climbs to his roof to leap after her, only the roof was shingled decades ago by his father, Harv, who by all accounts did a lousy job, two-foot shingles showing sixteen inches to the weather, and the rotten shingles give way beneath, and the rotten sheathing, and Jule Shellnut falls through the roof, landing in the bucket tub on top of his father, Harv, who, everyone agrees, gets what he deserves. Selvin Webb shouts, "Huzzah!" leaps off his roof, and lands in a pile of hay. His family watches from the roof—they all moan good-naturedly and each take their turn, Selvin's wife then son then daughter, and each time they hit the hay the family moans good-naturedly. "Maybe next year," they say, "God's will be praised." Remaining on the roof is Selvin's uncle, who insists on leaping from the opposite side of the house, where there's no hay. "Fools!" he shouts at them all. "God don't honor the faith of the faithless!" and he closes his eyes and leaps as high as he can—but not high enough, for he falls to the earth with a cry. Still this is no surprise, he picks himself up and limps inside, where he will set the break himself.

The Reverend Colonel hobbles over cobblestones to the cabin of Flora and Lutherly Grist and their son Algie. The villagers of Hiram pride themselves on their cleanliness and thrift, as well as their onions, but of these, only the latter is found at the Grist cabin—onion peels litter the floor, onions hang in bunches from the rafters, the bulbs sprouting unsightly growths. Flora offers the Reverend Colonel breakfast and he thanks her kindly but refuses. Flora is frying onions, the onion-pinched air stings the Reverend Colonel's eyes, as he informs her that he's come to bless them all for leaping. "Even Algie?" asks Flora, and the Reverend Colonel nods. "Algie can't leap," she says. "The wicked brute."

Her son Algie has just turned thirteen the week

before—leaping age. He sits in the corner, his chair leaning precariously against the wall, biting into an enormous onion like an apple. He says it will be great fun to go leaping.

"No," says Flora.

"But I leap off the ledge at the swimming hole."

"This is different."

"How?"

Flora looks to Lutherly to answer, who sits in the opposite corner, crippled with age, he can hardly see or hear but lives in a comfortable oblivion of memory, recalling the days when they rode sleds down the hills slick with pine needles, and they raided the ducks and carried them to the top of Knob Hill to watch them fly back frantic to the river, but this mischief-making doesn't compare to that of his son Algie, who breaks windows, who swipes clothes drying on the line, who sneaks into pastures and pushes over sleeping cows, unafraid of the brute-horned bulls. The cows fall and bellow, wind issuing loudly from their bowels. He steals dynamite from the mining crews and blasts brook trout out of the water holes, ears ringing for days. He ignores all authorities except his mother, whom he adores, and who now snatches at the Reverend Colonel's staff to prevent him from blessing Algie, from waggling it in his direction.

The Reverend Colonel looks at her, genial, indifferent, amused. "Everyone is allowed to leap," he says to Flora. "The Lord chooses who he must."

The fatback and onions crackle and sizzle but Flora pays the fryer no mind. She agitates easily, she can't help herself from shouting. "Four children," she shouts. "I had four children. Eula, Hughie, Herbert, Gus. Eula, Hughie, Herbert, Gus!" She repeats the names until she is hoarse, she shouts the names into the ear of the Reverend Colonel. Lutherly convulses in his seat, clears a log of phlegm from his throat, then falls back to sleep. The fatback and onions are burning black onto the pan and the room fills with smoke. The Reverend Colonel's eyes water, his white curly hair wilts. He withdraws his staff from Flora's grasp and explains that yes, he sees her predicament, God seems to have been selfish in regard to the Grists, one might indeed be tempted to think it unfair, but this is not so. It shouldn't surprise her to know that others regard her as lucky, her family blessed. For Flora did once have four children—Eula, Hughie, Herbert, Gus—and at age thirteen each of them leapt, and each was obliged. Flora, bereft, believed their virtue was to blame.

Late in age, she'd borne Algie, and raised him sin ridden, too heavy with iniquity to be lifted, repulsive to the hand of God. She never bathed him, never scolded, never required a minute's work. She cooked whatever he wanted, chicken and dumplings, grape pie, sweet corn pone with wild-cherry jelly. She'd slaughter a hog and he'd eat backbones and ribs for days. He rewarded her indulgence with exuberance. Her other children were faithful, careful creatures—they loved her with the same grateful, thoughtless devotion they loved the coats they wore in winter or the beds they slept in. But Algie's love was explosive. He never took her love for granted—never took anything for granted that wasn't in front of him. As a child he would wail every night when the sun went down, pointing at the sky and shouting. No one could convince him of its return until the morning, when he would jump from bed and run onto the porch, pointing at the sun and laughing. He loved his mother with the same extravagance— when she returned home from her labors, he would take her hands and dance her round the yard with glee, kicking up dust. Once when she fell ill with fever, he walked a dozen miles and broke into Orly LeMint's mansion, ignoring the sterling silver and the engraved gemstones but going straight to the cellar, from which he stole a hunk of ice for his mother. Nearly all of it was melted by the time he got back to Hiram, but he gave the shard of ice to her proudly, like a cat with its kill. He cared little for what heaven might be had in the skies, his joy was for the things of the earth: its dirt, its girth.

Algie finishes eating the onion and picks up an old backbone for gnawing, eyeing the Reverend Colonel's wooden leg as if it might be next. The Reverend Colonel suggests a parable might be in order. Flora tells him there will be no parables, no blessings, no leaping, no business at all with God and his ways. "You hear that?" she turns and says to Algie. "No leaping!"

"Yes, Mama," says Algie.

"No leaping!" says Flora to the Reverend Colonel, and opens the door, waiting for him to leave. The Reverend Colonel only smiles quizzically and points his staff at Algie, "Even the wicked will not be forgotten on Leaping Day," he says, and exits the Grist cabin out into the bright damp florescent spring morning, where, on the other side of the closed cabin door, he waggles his staff and sprinkles a handful of dust, to bless the boy for leaping. When he is done, he looks up and sees Algie leering at him from the hillock of refuse behind the Grist cabin. Algie shakes his head and waves his finger as if it is the Reverend Colonel who is naughty, whereas it is he who has just climbed out the window, and he who hurries away as Flora bursts out the back door, calling for him.

Lawton Dickey has climbed with his sister to the top of the tower, an open-air platform fifty feet high without barrier or rail. Lawton can see for miles from here, just above the needles of the longleaf pines, the undying country, the sprawling thickets of wiregrass, sheathed in rust, the alabaster blossoms among the green and vibrant spring, the glimmering blur of a body of water beyond. The sun almost directly overhead, casting no shadows. A silent flurry of gnats, and the occasional hovering bird of prey. The air seems more humid this high, Lawton blinks against the blaring heat but his sister doesn't blink nor does she pause to admire the view. She has worn her best for the occasion, ankle-length dress homespun from her finest white calico and blooming peach-blossom hat and new lace-up shoes all the way from Iamonia, the flesh of her face freshly oiled, and the flesh of her hands and arms. Lawton imagines her basted and baking like a Cornish hen. She proceeds fearlessly to the tower edge, surveying the villagers below and their foolish leaping.

Lawton says, "You leap first, I'll leap second."

"Me, a rheumatic," she says. "What kind of leaper would I be?"

According to her own calculations, thinks Lawton, this seems beside the point—what kind of leaper was his father, who hardly leapt at all, but stood, twenty years ago, high at the tower's edge, palms raised to God like a prophet, and he called out something harsh and definitive and inscrutable, he did not leap but dove headfirst like a skilled diver, hitting the earth with a smack like the slap of a paddle.

Lawton asks his sister, "What do you think happened to Father after he died?"

"Heaven," she says, "what else?" The sunlight shines blinding bright off the oily fat of her flesh.

"Then what good is leaping?" asks Lawton. He wears his father's overalls, which his sister has pressed with the hot stone, hemmed the seams, polished the buckles. The overalls have no need of a belt but he wears one anyway, his lucky belt with the horseshoe buckle. He has left his candy mints on the assumption there would be no need but now regrets it, mouth dry and full of dust. "If the dead find their way to heaven, same as the obliged, why the leaping?"

"Not *all* dead end up in heaven, you fool," she says. "Father did because he leapt from the tower. And that's the only chance your devil's soul will ever get—the leap of faith turns sinner to saint. You, reading those filthy letters and writing them, too, prying into every sinner's business." And she explains that he is to wait at the top, she will circulate among the villagers and draw their attention to the tower.

"Is that necessary?" asks Lawton.

"That's the point," she says. "An example to others." And she makes her way stiffly down the stairs. Lawton crawls on hands and knees, careful of splinters, to the platform's edge, better to observe the leapers, who are leaping off the rooftops, they leap with honest joy and abandon, shouting out to God and leaping, singing the leaping hymns and throwing back the bottle. Lawton watches his neighbor Brace Guthrie take a running start from the ridge of his roof and leap gracefully off the precipice, arms spread like an eagle. Brace's drunken brother tries the same trick but lacks his brother's style, he stumbles and tumbles off the edge, landing flat on his back. He doesn't get up. The villagers toss infants into the air and catch them. Some linger on their rooftops all day, drinking and dancing and singing, leaping then falling then climbing to the roof to leap again. Even the elderly are leaping. There goes Old Strickly—he sits on the edge of the roof and hangs his legs over and eases off the edge as if into a tub. He falls to the earth but soon is on his feet again, dazed, limping, it is just as Lawton's sister said, even the old folks will risk broken bones for a ticket to heaven. But Lawton wonders, What's so great about heaven anyhow? The distant cowbells sound like dull wedding bells, an eagle hovers above, the gnats wobble in their crazed agitations, the leapers shout with laughter. How could heaven be any better than this?

And then there is Octie Bogue and Magaline, who stand at the edge of their roof, strapped, straddling the harness, Magaline holding on to Octie's back. "When I say *leap*, we leap," says Octie.

Magaline glances at the small crowd that has gathered in the scrap-and-grass enclosure of their yard. She waves and calls out hello, then hisses at Octie, "This is silly!"

"Don't you love me?" asks Octie.

"Why can't we just hold hands?" asks Magaline.

"When I say *leap*, we leap," says Octie. They practice simultaneous knee bends, then suddenly Octie shouts, "Leap!" and he leaps, only Magaline doesn't leap, and Octie tumbles off the roof roped to the immobile Magaline and she tips over with his falling weight and tumbles after. Some in the crowd gasp and others guffaw but they don't guffaw for long: the couple is caught as if by an invisible hand and lifted into the sky, until their rise is halted.

"Hellfire!" shouts Octie.

"Octie!" shouts Magaline, as they hang suspended thirty feet high, clasped together and dangling for all to see, like mythical figures caught in the act of illicit congress and made an example to the world.

The villagers have seen plenty but they've never seen this and they quickly come running. "What're they caught on?" asks Wiley Cooper, the beekeeper.

"Caught on nothing," says Grady Merkel.

"Somebody get my lasso," says Wiley, "and we'll haul them down."

"Can't haul down somebody obliged," says Grady.

"That's not obliged," says Wiley. "That's stuck."

"Could be obliged," says Grady. "Just taking longer than ordinary."

"Hello?" calls out Wiley to Octie and Magaline. "Can you hear?"

"Hellfire!" shouts Octie. Octie and Magaline kick and grimace, they wag their arms as if trying to fly, hanging there neither sinking nor ascending but dangling in the sky as if on a string. "Somebody tell us how we're supposed to do this!" shouts Octie.

"Get the reverend," someone says, but the Reverend Colonel has already arrived, has been watching for some time, his arms crossed on his chest, unimpressed by even this, and they ask what should be done and he offers another parable: *Two soldiers are both killed in battle and go to heaven. One sings for joy. The other weeps. "Why are you weeping?" asks the one. "It's not what I expected," says the other.* Meanwhile a villager has retrieved Wiley's rope, they form it into a lasso and hurl it toward the couple but it's not long enough and someone strikes out in search of another.

"I will not be roped and hauled down like a heifer!" says Magaline to Octie.

"What the hell else are we supposed to do?" says Octie.

"Undo the buckles," says Magaline.

"Magaline!" says Octie.

"Undo the buckles!"

"Hellfire!"

Magaline pulls at the buckles. Octie tries to stop her but she pulls the buck knife from his back pocket and savagely cuts at the rope holding him to her, he tries to turn in the harness to stop her but he is bound facing forward and she cuts through the rope. She cuts the last rope and the harness falls and Octie falls, too, while Magaline lingers in the air. Octie snatches hold of her foot but she is seized with the desire for rising. "Forget it, mister!" she shouts, kicks her foot free, and rises heavenward. She laughs, tickled, as Octie cries out one last time, and the crowd cheers and clears the way for Octie's fall.

Several have broken bones and a few have been obliged: Jeptha Sanders, Maude Shope, and little Rob Echols, son of Sheldon Echols, just four feet tall, fourteen years old. Esco Duckett has heard of these villagers obliged and is all the more ready to undertake his own leap, having arranged to negate his broken-ankle luck by rolling a neighbor's rotting buckboard full of hay underneath his roof to provide cushion in the event of a fall. He stands on the edge of his slope roof and Beulah sits on the roof ridge leaning against the chimney holding one of the little ones.

Beulah says, "Thirty-six chickens. Six acres onion. Four head cattle. Three bawling mouths to feed. And you have no shame."

"Don't you fear for my ankles, I told you about that wagon."

"You don't have the luck to land in a wagon."

"And you don't have the good sense to leave a husband be. Ever heard of Jonah? A man knows when God is calling."

"Which is it I'm supposed to hope for? Esco broke another ankle, or Esco gone to God?"

"Maybe my wife showed a pinch more piety, God'd respect my efforts."

"Can't you find some other way to play at your prayers that don't ruin your family?"

Esco removes his rumpled billycock hat, bows, and says, "Beulah, take care of yourself." He replaces the hat on his head, turns back to the roof's edge, confirms the buckboard underneath, and swings both arms, rocking forward and calling to God to sit up and take note, here comes Esco, then he leaps, with his swollen belly and flapping arms and fine striped wool blazer blowing out in the breeze, leaping desperate and ungainly like a lamed barnyard fowl trying to take flight, only noticing once it's too late the scalawag Algie Grist crouching behind the buckboard. Algie springs up as soon as Esco's feet leave the roof and he gives the buckboard a shove and it rolls off down the hill. Esco hardly manages to gain any height by virtue of his own leaping strength, there is no arc at all, plummeting to the earth as he has always plummeted and landing on his heels, stiff as a plank, and he jackknifes and crumples to the ground, clutching his ankles, rolling in the dirt and howling in pain. The villagers are accustomed to such and pay him no mind.

The Reverend Colonel hobbles over to Esco and says, "Sure now. Don't you worry. Those ankles will heal up real smart, soon as the tillage is done."

Beulah climbs down from the roof, bawling quietly into

her shawl. The Reverend Colonel offers to help Beulah carry Esco inside but she refuses. "Shush," she says to Esco. "You better shush," and she pulls him up by the arms and drags him inside limp like a slaughtered calf. Flora arrives breathless and sweating, chest heaving, looking for her boy Algie. The Reverend Colonel shrugs. Beulah hears Flora outside her cabin and comes charging out, still bawling, she marches up to Flora and slaps her. "Don't I have enough hard luck?" she bawls at Flora. "Don't I?"

Flora stands there, stunned. "What's my boy done?" she says.

"That's no boy but some kind of animal," says Beulah.

"What awful thing has he hauled off and done?" asks Flora.

"He comes round here again, he's got trouble," says Beulah. "We got four mink traps and two bear traps and I'll set every one with bait for that animal of yours."

"You see?" says Flora to the Reverend. "He's got no business leaping."

"Oh I don't know," says the Reverend. "Perhaps that would be just the thing."

Feasting and drinking and merrymaking, impromptu fiddle music sounding scurrilously from the rooftops, villagers dancing and cutting the pigeonwing. Five leapers obliged, counting Magaline Bogue, giving cause for hope for heaven for another year. Life was nothing to complain about anyhow, life on the first Sunday in spring, the buds blooming, the fresh sprouts of sugarcane grown high overhead, sturgeon leaping out of the Omanockee, the loamy sod giving itself to the till—but now here is Lawton Dickey's sister, with her best homespun calico dress and peach-blossom hat and squeaking-new lace-up shoes, a sweet-rose cordial in a bootleg-liquor hamlet. Isn't it going to be something to see now, she proclaims, Lawton Dickey leaping from that great height, leaping into the bosom of God, and won't it be a sight now, everyone drop your fiddles and come on over to the tower, you'll see a proof of faith to put the village to shame, my brother, Lawton, leaping from fifty feet above. The villagers do as told, they look up straight into the blinding sun and see what must be Lawton, clinging on hands and knees to the tower's edge. "Hold on, Lawton! I'm coming!" shouts Wiley Cooper. "Is he going to leap or just stay up there tickling Jesus by the toes?" asks Selvin Webb, and the crowd howls laughing, they've been waiting for Lawton to leap from the tower for years, but they're willing to gather and goad him on for a good time, knowing he'll never do it, and who could blame him? His father had gone too far with that business. They're men of faith, not fanatics. They wear mud caps and rough denim trousers, the women in sack skirts belted tight about the waist with cord. The fiddlers fiddle a rowdy leaping song and the villagers cut the pigeonwing, the boys leaping from the rooftops for the fun of it, into their father's arms.

Flora Grist returns from her search among the onion fields calling out for her son, pushing through the crowd, until she bumps into Lawton's sister, and Flora asks if she's

seen Algie. Lawton's sister replies that Flora has no reason
to worry—God knows where her son is.

"That's what I'm worried about!" shouts Flora. "He already
hauled off four of mine."

"That's blasphemy," says Lawton's sister.

"Eula, Hughie, Herbert, Gus!" shouts Flora.

"They're better with God than the likes of you," says
Lawton's sister.

"What do you know of God?" says Flora. "God's got
nothing to do with you—and me neither!"

"For God so loved the world," says Lawton's sister, "that
he gave his only begotten son."

"He can do what he wants with *his* son," says Flora, "but
he better keep his hands off mine."

"We must all sacrifice ourselves to righteousness," says
Lawton's sister.

"The only self you aim to sacrifice is your brother," says
Flora. "And that's not a sacrifice for you at all."

Lawton's sister flinches, which disturbs the haughty angle
of her peach-blossom hat. She stares at Flora then adjusts the
hat. "You just watch and see," says Lawton's sister. "You just
watch Lawton leap off that tower and see," and she points
to the top of the tower, only Lawton can no longer be seen,
he has grown dizzy with the height and crawled back to the
center of the tower. He would crawl back down the stairs but
can't face the ridicule of the villagers, his sister's scorn. If he
waits here long enough, he'll get caught in a squall, possibly
lightning will strike, a preferable end.

"Ho, ho, ho," says a voice behind him, "what's this?" It is the boy Algie Grist. Lawton suspects that the boy means to do him harm—goad him into leaping or push him off. There is a wild unpredictability to his gestures, his eyes. A witless brute, a fool's fool. Still there is something fresh and unaccountable to his face, something brotherly in the freckles and impetuous grin, a turbulent, insectile intelligence. He is a head taller than Lawton, he wears stolen overalls two sizes too small, high above his ankles. This bothers Lawton: not that the boy steals clothes, but that they don't fit. Lawton tries to casually crawl back from the boy. The boy stands still at the top of the stairs with his impetuous grin. Lawton unbuckles his lucky belt in case he might need it, his only weapon.

"This is my tower," says the boy. "But you can stay if you follow orders. Know how to follow orders?"

"All too well," says Lawton.

"Good." The boy digs his finger into his ear, thinking, then says, "I can't come up with any orders. You think of some then I'll give them to you."

Lawton has removed his belt, but perhaps, he thinks, he won't need it after all. A simple ruse might suffice. "I guess you came up here on account of you wanted to leap," says Lawton.

"Sure," says Algie. "Looks like fun."

"Not at all," says Lawton. "It's dangerous. Could be deadly."

"Even more fun," says Algie.

"Could be," says Lawton. "But only if you do it right."

"No right way or wrong way. Just leaping."

"Not at all," says Lawton. "If you're not careful, you'll be obliged."

"That's no fun," says Algie.

"So listen carefully," says Lawton, "and I'll give your orders."

"Hold on," says the boy. "*I'm* giving orders."

"Yes," says Lawton. "I forgot. This is what I want you to tell us to do." And he gives the boy instructions, while he can hear the shouts of his sister below, she is growing angry, accusing the villagers of a false faith, accusing Lawton as well, she shouts at him to come on out to the edge of the tower, to show himself in his righteousness and the righteousness of their father before he takes his leap. But Lawton does not appear, and the villagers make more wisecracks. Wiley Cooper asks if Lawton wants to borrow his angel wings and they all guffaw. Someone calls for the opinion of the Reverend Colonel, at the back of the crowd, leaning against the railing at LaRowe's Dry Goods, looking amiable and disinterested like a stranger in need of a favor but with no inclination to ask, his curly white hair and white mustache gone white long before his time, good leg propped on the step so that all his weight is borne unnaturally on the wooden peg, which has the curious effect of making him seem to float. He does not move or seem to address any one of them in particular as he offers another parable: *Two great armies faced each other, they fought all day and night, three days and three nights, and lo, when the sun rose on the fourth day, only one was left standing. "What will become of me?" he cried. And he fell upon his sword.* The Reverend Colonel stops talking and points to the top of the tower, where Lawton, it seems, has finally found his way to the tower's edge, or the villagers assume it is Lawton, in truth it is difficult to tell, for the sun shines directly above like the white-hot eye of God, and all that can be made of the figure is his shimmering outline, and the tower casts no shadow, as if it didn't exist, no clouds in the sky, and the tumbledown shacks and cabins of Hiram shimmer in the bright hot noontime light like a mirage, while a figure stands at the tower's edge with arms extended like a prophet, silent, and the prophet that might be Lawton does not leap but dives headfirst like a skilled diver, and the villagers barely have time to stumble out of the way before he hits the ground with a smack like a paddle. The body does not move. The villagers do not move. The body caught in violent contortion like the twisted steel from some mad blacksmith's forge, face hidden in the spring-green grass, blood pooling and seeping into the earth.

"Lawton!" cries Lawton's sister, greased face blazing in the glare of the sun, and she faints and falls.

No one moves to help her. Gladys Pitts says to her husband, Rufus, "Those your overalls?"

"Might be," says Rufus.

Gladys says, "Some gall. Leaping in another man's pants."

"Only that's not Lawton Dickey," says Wiley Cooper, and just then they hear a scream of grief. It is Flora Grist, who has finally fought through the crowd, and she stumbles to the body of Algie Grist and falls beside it. She takes the limp hand in her hands and wails, rocking on her knees over the body. The villagers bump and shuffle in startled consternation if not grief. The men stern and earnest, hands plunged deep in pockets, clearing their throats. The women whisper harshly under their breaths, they daub their faces with coarse denim bandannas. It was a damn fool idea anyway, that tower, didn't God tear down Babel for a reason? Flora curses God, she curses the Reverend Colonel, she curses Lawton Dickey and his cataleptic sister, she curses the village, she looks at them each who will not return her stare and calls them to account for the death of her child.

"Well, hell," says Wiley Cooper, "we didn't push him off or nothing."

"Come on home, Flora," says Monroe Gibbs. "Come on and let's get home."

"Home," says Flora. "My boy was my home."

"Come on," says Monroe Gibbs, who was kissed by the widow Darlie Sewell, always a gentle way with women. He touches her on the elbow but she does not move, he tries to lift her by the elbow but she does not move, kneeling over her son, who was blessed by the Reverend Colonel but to no good end, his face hidden in the blood-thatched grass. They have ignored Lawton's sister but now she stirs, peach-blossom hat knocked cockeyed in the fall, moaning and clutching her side as if the pain of her brother's supposed death could be isolated in her ribs. Wiley explains to her that it's not her brother but Algie Grist that leapt and died. She sits up, leaning back against the rough-hewn log wall of the tower. "Not Lawton?" she says, her shining face blanching white, blond eyebrows vanishing, nothing to hide the heavy, livid, lidless eyes. Where is he, she demands, her chicken-livered brother, and why didn't he leap?

The villagers say he must've slipped away when no one was looking.

"Maybe he was obliged," someone offers.

"Not likely," says Wiley. "I believe God requires you to leap first."

She rises on trembling legs, leaning against the wall of the tower before wandering off in search of her brother, the crowd parting for her like cleaved sea waters.

They leave Flora there, kneeling over the body, the afternoon is getting late and nothing more can be done, it is Leaping Day after all. They might be forgiven if they indulge in a bit of liquor, they may not fiddle or sing out of respect for the dead, but they might partake of the griddle cakes and the fisherman's stew, simmering on the fire for days. They cannot be expected to mourn for the boy, who tormented them with his devilish ways. He was never right in the mind, they say, he had no business in Hiram anyhow. They are not righteous, perhaps, but they are reasonable, and they will pursue their celebrations in joyless disturbed incongruity. And so no one sees Flora Grist rise in the twilight from her son's contorted body and enter through the tower door and climb the stairs to the top—no one but the Reverend

Colonel, who has retained his position at LaRowe's Dry Goods, and who observes Flora's movements with the detached abstract wonderment peculiar to such faithless men of faith, who have long since learned the folly of our vanity and toil but cannot help but find some comfort in the witness of it, all human activity one long compromise between honor and horror. The Reverend Colonel watches Mother Grist climb the tower, knowing what she intends to do. She finds there the ridiculous figure of Lawton Dickey tied with his own belt to the post, whimpering, an onion shoved into his mouth. The belt was Lawton's idea but the onion was Algie's, which Lawton protested but which, tied to the post, he couldn't resist. He cannot think of any worse fate, other than leaping, his mouth filled with the abhorrent inedible onion, like a calcified tumor, teeth clenched into the oily skin, eyes burning with tears so that he could not even see the boy fall to his death. But Flora Grist knows better—when she finds him bound at the top of the tower, she releases him from his ignorance though not his bondage. She informs him that his life is not worth the fear it has caused him. And she leaps off the tower into the swelling immoderate darkness not to be obliged but to meet her son in oblivion. Only in the eternal perversity of nature she is obliged, rising into the night against her will, rising as her four children rose, Eula, Hughie, Herbert, and Gus. But the thought of reunion with these brings her no comfort, they have no need for her, and so she is the first in the long chronicle of the obliged to rise not laughing but wailing, which none but the Reverend Colonel is available to witness.

"Sure now," he thinks. "Won't that make a fine parable, Mother Grist gone to God," the wisp of her figure rising in the dark like ash on the wind.

DEATH OF THE OARSMAN

It was my father that was the oarsman, and the last there ever was.

We believed no one could die on our island, the gods forbade it, and disaster would follow. And so when the sickness came upon one of us, the oarsman would row away with the dying islander over the horizon. My father the oarsman and his father before and his father and on and on. No one knew where he went, and no one knew what became of the bodies, but the bark was always empty when my father rowed it back to shore. Some said he floated somewhere over the horizon, waiting for the dying to die, and then heaved the body into the sea. But most imagined there was a place, a watery grave, a shining coral garden among the darker waters, where the bodies could be released and remain. Some said the released didn't die at all, but lived in peace on the Island of the Blessed, and we would each meet them at the end of the oarsman's journey. As for my father, he laughed at such stories, and would wink at me, and tell the villagers of something called the East Stream, which carried the bodies away. "Ah!" someone would say. "The East Stream!" and the villagers would laugh, for they knew Father was a sly one. As for me, I tried not to speculate. The mind can imagine anything, but that doesn't make it so.

The villagers always expressed much respect for Father, giving him gifts to win his favor, for a swift and successful journey, when their own day came. My father took pride in these gifts even as he knew them to be a bribe. "A bribe for what?" he would say. "So I will dump their corpses from the right side of the boat, not the left!" And he would hold up his newest treasure, a block of rock salt or the finest dried haddock or pheasant eggs still warm from the roost. "You see," my father would say, "stupidity has a price, which they will keep paying their entire lives." He rarely shared these gifts, an old man must enjoy his few remaining pleasures, he said, smiling, while I was a young man, and would receive my own gifts, too, in time, when I took his place. But I did not wish to wait for that time, and dreaded to think of it, and stole a pheasant egg when Father wasn't looking. I didn't think he noticed, but now I am not sure, for he noticed everything, and enjoyed testing my own powers of observation. "Did you happen to observe," he would ask, "what was different today about your Aunt Milori?" And he would point out that on her neck there grew a brand-new wart. That the Midwife had two broken fingernails. That my friend Crale couldn't smell. That the widow Auramine was left-handed, and didn't know it. I tried to observe similar things and report them to Father—Milori's wart had grown three hairs, her husband, Stammel, was missing a tooth. This pleased him, and I felt proud, though I saw no point in observing such things. It was true Milori's wart had grown bigger, but I knew Milori herself was the same, who always took my hand in hers but resisted all other contact, who loved to cook but disliked eating, who was frequently ill but never came down with the sickness. Milori was Milori, no matter how many warts she grew. And my father was my father, the oarsman, who grew stronger and more confident with the days, the fine wrinkles beside his eyes lifting with his smile, and strong, taut arms while other fathers grew soft and wan. Some said he might live another decade or more, some said he might live on without end, like our ancestors, and I wanted to believe them, though I knew people will say anything, for their own reasons. They say women with harelips shouldn't grow potatoes. They say you shouldn't eat salt fish on a full moon. They say the Midwife likes to sleep at night with the Crier. They say short boys climb the tallest trees. And they say long ago there was no need for the bark, nor the oarsman: the people of our island never died. They say the women were collecting sea urchins when they came upon him—a stranger—collapsed, naked, beaten by the sea onto the beach. No evidence of a boat; they said he swam to us from over the horizon. The women revived him and helped him to the market, where the villagers tried to question him but grew fearful of his strange speech and insisted he leave. By sundown he had been put in a scow and pushed off to sea, but they say it was too late—his age was contagious—and in years to come the villagers began dying with the sickness, the abject flesh and craven face and eyes lost behind a milk-white haze, and age for our island ever since. But my father never liked this story, and said the mistake was not in the welcome offered the stranger but in shoving him off to sea. "May I ask if that is how we should treat strangers?" he said, ever formal in his speech, even with me, and yet with his body he was more comfortable, and he stretched out his cold feet to warm by the fire. "May I ask if that is how we should face what we think to be our dangers?"

We did not face many dangers, only boreal winds blowing the thatch clean free from our roofs, or summer sand wasps, or a moon bear surprised with her cubs. Or the danger of childbirth, which was how I lost my own mother. My father was called for all births, and the Midwife, too. The Midwife oared the mother out to sea in one bark, and my father oared out in another, and we watched them from the shore. No one knew what had happened until the end: the Midwife returned with mother and child, or with motherless child, or childless mother, or alone, while my father oared over the horizon with his charge. It was said when he oared away with Mother he didn't return for a week, but I didn't believe it. He wouldn't neglect his duty for that long.

Aunt Milori watched over me when Father was called. She loved my father but loved to mock him, too, her only brother. She was the only one who treated him with anything less than respect. "Oh, I'll never be a man, not in a million years," she said, "with their vanities, their cold hands and vanities," sucking her teeth and laughing in hoarse, throaty gasps. She asked what kind of man was it that everyone loved, but who himself loved no one? That knew the secrets of the sea, but kept them to himself, so they did no one any good? My aunt suffered from many ailments, and couldn't resist comparing herself to Father, healthy for all his days. One morning, as she sat and cracked walnuts against the table, and I sat next to her, eating them, she complained of carbuncles, laughing at herself, who could barely sweep the floor in the morning. She asked me to carry in a fresh load of wood and told me to stack it under the window, unlike Stammel, who never listened, who always stacked it too close to the bed, and the wood brought bugs. "Well, what a lot of wood," she said, "in only one trip, just like your father!" She asked how old I was, and seemed surprised when I told her fourteen. Such a good boy, such an excellent boy, but not a boy at all, but a young man, and wasn't it time my father put me to work? Many boys worked in their family gardens, growing turnips and potatoes, but my father had no garden, relying on the generosity of others. Other boys began fishing the sea with their fathers, but my father never fished, and only went to sea when a villager came down with the sickness, and was ready to be released. I asked my aunt what work I could do, and she said I might assist my father as oarsman.

"But that's not allowed," I said. "Not until he's sick, and I row him out to sea, and then I take his place."

She laughed, oh yes, that was certainly true, but why should a healthy young man be left idle, and besides, she had her own secret, if I cared to hear it. She cracked another walnut and spoke what was for her a whisper, but a regular voice for the rest of us, and she flashed her leafy teeth and told me the people of the island were getting sick more quickly. Who knew when the next islander would succumb?

Some poor soul's eyes gone milk white with the sickness, and Father away with another. How terrible it was to be released to sea, but more terrible to die on the island like some filthy animal. I reassured her my father was never gone long, usually only a few hours, occasionally a night. She gathered the soft pulps of nuts into a sack and swept the shells onto the floor. "My poor nephew!" she said. "Only thirteen years old, what does he know of anything, and still his sick aunt badgers him, only just a boy!"

That afternoon I thought with dread about my aunt's suggestion—oaring the dead out into the empty nothing of the sea. But I knew my dread had less to do with the death of any particular villager and more to do with Father's, returning without him, and without him on and on. Now Milori suggested this did not have to be, I could work alongside him rather than replace him, and of course I was fourteen, not thirteen, and old enough to learn the ways of the sea. Perhaps it was true, what the villagers said, that there might be some shining coral garden over the horizon, or an Island of the Blessed, and I dreamed of arriving there with a bouquet of moon-blue cornflowers and handing them to Mother.

When I arrived home, Father had not returned. I wandered the forest, walking up to the Whistle Cliffs, searching the horizon for his bark. But he didn't return until the next day, when I found him at the table, warming his hands in a bowl of water. His hands went numb when exposed to a chill, and numb out there on the open sea. I watched as the color returned to his hands in the water, his bone-white fingers flushing a deep mottled purple under the skin with blood. A fire was lit in the hearth, which Father always kept burning to warm his hands and feet, even in summer, when on the warmest nights I would sleep in the clearing to escape the heat. He was usually tired when he returned from the sea, but would ask how I was, and how was Stammel, and Milori. I would tell him of Milori's troubles, and we would eat and spend the rest of the night in silence. But on this afternoon he didn't ask after Stammel or Milori, but was easily agitated, and grew angry when he saw I had not cut logs for the wood-pile. I said I'd spent the day looking after Milori—she wasn't well. "When is that woman ever well?" he said. "Haven't you ever noticed this, my sister is never well?" Of course I had noticed this, but I said nothing. Father tore off a piece of salt fish. He ate quickly and became impatient if I did not eat quickly, too, and so I chewed slowly, and picked the head for myself, which I knew he liked best. Father asked what did Milori complain of this morning, and I told him.

"All right," he said, "but what is a carbuncle?"

I said nothing, chewing slowly.

"A carbuncle," he said, "is a blister filled with pus, as it were. Have you ever observed on my sister any blisters filled with pus?"

I had never observed blisters on Milori, but I did observe something else—my father was not being consistent: he claimed I never observed anything, and so if I never observed blisters on his sister, this only proved my failure, not hers.

Should I point this contradiction out to him? It might win the argument, but it was my own secret, an observation I had made that, if shared, would no longer belong to me. The knowledge made me stronger, and him weaker, and I kept quiet the rest of the meal, sleeping that night in the clearing. The next day I saw Milori and searched her arms, face, and ankles for carbuncles. I didn't see any, but I didn't care. The sicker she felt, the more she laughed, with her hoarse, throaty gasps. We laughed about the stupid things Stammel did, how he slept in nothing but wool cap and socks, and woke every morning with his ridiculous prick. At home, Father remained distracted, showing no interest in Milori's troubles, and so I cared little for his, sulking at the Whistle Cliffs, and sleeping every night, though cold, out in the clearing. Father was not called over the next few days, and spent his time as usual, talking among the villagers at market, or visiting their homes, blessing them with his presence and proudly bringing home their gifts. He began chopping wood again, my task, but one he performed more efficiently, splitting the logs in one blow.

And then one day he was called to sea, and again he was away two nights instead of one, and wet with rain when he returned. Again he kept silent, warming his hands in the steaming water for hours, and I stoked the fire to heat the water for the bowls. At last I asked what happened. He didn't answer, and the steam softened his beard and brow. "Who is it you know," he asked, "that enjoys the hard work of living? And yet these fools want to go on living, though they hate the work of it, and not a soul is grateful when I carry them away.

But why should that surprise me?" That was when I offered to help him, there was no reason he had to work alone, together we could share the burden, I said, if he taught me how.

Father considered. "This is Milori's idea?"

"Yes."

"And you intend to have *two* oarsmen, as it were."

"Yes."

"Then why not three? Why not four or five?"

I said nothing.

"Why not allow any idiot fisherman with a scow," said Father, "to carry the dead to sea?" He ran his wet hands through his hair. The fire blazed in the pit, and the dry pine cracked and tumbled into a heap of burning coal. It all burned away in flames, these good intentions, my face glowing hot by the fire, cursing myself for trying to help, and hating my father for denying it. His hands were rawboned and withered, not a father's hands, too long in the hot water. That was the first I saw them shaking. I told him he was getting old. I said this to confirm it as a fact that I myself must understand—but I also meant to belittle him.

"Yes?" he said. "Is this the brilliant thing you've observed? You're ready to be done with me, but why am I surprised?"

"I never want to be done with you."

"Just a child. Think of it—a child hauling corpses across the sea!"

"Someday you'll have to teach me."

"Milori uses you to placate her own fears."

I said she was his sister, but he said she was just a tired old woman, who was afraid of what the days would bring, but this was nothing original, he said, every old woman is afraid, and in the end he was responsible for them all. Did I know, he asked, what I was offering? A gift isn't generous when the giver doesn't understand what he gives. Innocence deserves to be protected, said Father. They want what they will wish they never had. Did I think these people died quietly? The sea nothing but gentle waves, a cool breeze? Did I think the villagers would admire me when I became the oarsman? Wasn't that what I really wanted—to be admired? "They think they admire you," he said, "but in the end it is you whom they despise."

Early spring—summer in the afternoons, quick to winter in the evenings, and the forsythia blooming, the petals falling away, green leaves sprouting in their place. My father, too, was changing—eating less and sleeping less, his cold, rawboned hands grown hard and knotty, swelling at the knuckles and trembling, like the gnarled branches of pine shuddering in the wind at the height of the Whistle Cliffs. To learn the ways of the sea, when Father was gone I began oaring out with my friends Crale and Rine, fishermen, who taught me how to tack against the tides, and pull with legs and arms instead of the back, and how to hold the oars to avoid blisters. I often wondered whether Milori was right, if the villagers were getting sick more quickly, for it seemed Father was away more often, sometimes one night, sometimes two, until one day he oared out to release the elder Damson, and did not return for two nights, then three. The villagers worried, some argued a search party should be sent, others protested no one but the oarsman was allowed beyond the horizon, these were matters we did not understand. Waiting is our only choice, they argued, and the majority agreed.

I no longer stayed at Aunt Milori's when Father was called, but remained alone at our cottage. Each morning Father was away, Milori sent Stammel with fresh eggs and a persimmon for my breakfast, but on the fifth day Father was gone with Damson, Stammel didn't bring fresh eggs and a persimmon, but news that Milori had the sickness, her eyes lost to the milk-white haze, she could hardly see a thing. We hurried to her cottage. Through the trees, I heard her crying. The warm morning sun shone through the needles of the pines. On her bed, in a dream, she cried out, and clawed at invisible bugs, blood on her nails. She wore her best dress, now fouled, wrists and ankles wasted to bone, her belly bloated obscenely, big as a squid. She stared through the milk-white glaze and held her bloated belly. She cried out for the Midwife, her belly was ready to give birth, why should an old woman be cursed with a child? Stammel sat still, hunched, hands resting on his walking stick, hair blown to white wisps of nothing. I asked what should be done, but he only stared back silently—the decision was up to me, the son of the oarsman. "Go," he said finally. "Where?" I asked, and he shrugged. I ran to the Midwife's, but the Midwife said there was nothing she could do, and looked at me as if I asked her to bring back the living from the dead. "The poor woman deserves some comfort!" I said.

"What do I know about a thing like that?"

I ran back to Father's house, hoping he might have returned. Crale found me there, the villagers were stirring, he said, what was I going to do? I thought of Milori dying on the island, like an animal, and I thought of Father away at sea. Why had he not returned? He's testing me, I told myself, though I only half believed it, and I told Crale I would take Milori out to sea. Crale crossed his arms in disbelief. "Father taught me the way," I lied. "He told me everything."

Crale scowled, but agreed to do as I asked, to send Rine to help at Milori's, and to furnish a scow with provisions. Rine and I carried her down the mossy shale, and Stammel limped with his stick behind. At the wharf the scow was ready, the oars in their locks, a blanket for Milori, two flagons of water, a flagon of wine, a sack of salt fish. We laid her in the scow and she cried out again for the Midwife. The villagers stood crowded on the stone wharf looking down at us, murmuring. I scanned the horizon, thinking Father might still arrive in time. The villagers scanned with me, hoping the same. But I had learned from Crale and Rine how to handle the oars, and I climbed into the scow and was pushed off to sea. Stammel stared after us, and the murmuring crowd. The waves beat against the beach and I rowed to overcome them.

We were alone on the sea. Milori slept fitfully, rocking on the gentle waves. I quickly grew tired, though the island was still visible, the pale face of the Whistle Cliffs shimmering like a memory in the distance. Milori lay sprawled before me, the foul bladder of her body, eyes glazed, breathing. I tried to cover her with the blanket, but it was moth-eaten and of meager size. When I placed the sack of salt fish under her head, she woke, suddenly, and stared at me terrified. "Who are you?" she said. I sat still, like some crawling insect that's been detected. Then I pulled my cap over my ears and resumed oaring. Sweat soaked her dress. Her belly was swollen bigger, and the bones of her bare ankles, her rotting teeth. "Who are you?" she whispered again, soft now, like the whisper of others.

"I'm the Midwife," I said. "And I'm rowing you out to sea."

"Ah, the Midwife," she said and laughed. I gave her some wine and resumed oaring, the Whistle Cliffs disappearing from view. The sun shone brightly now nearly overhead and the oars slapped the surface of the sea. A breeze blew from the west. My aunt lay calmly in the prow. I was pleased with my simple deception and rowed more confidently, taking pleasure in the work, pulling the oars into my chest and exhaling big breaths. Like an orphan, I thought, alone with nothing and no one on the great, empty sea. And then it occurred to me that out there I might find my father. I thought how angry he might be, but when he heard my story, he would be proud, to see his son oaring alone and without fear across the sea. My aunt groaned, no more oaring, she said, it's here I'll give birth. I gave her more wine, which she gulped like a child, but the wine quieted her only a few moments, she moaned louder, and demanded to know where we were going.

"To the Island of the Blessed," I said.

"Oh," she said, "Where is that?" Eyeing me, so I thought she'd returned to her senses.

"We follow the East Stream," I said.

"And the child will be born there?"

"Yes," I said, "among the blessed." She seemed so comforted by this lie that I took some comfort from it, too, and oared on under the sun, strong in the rhythm of the oars, hopeful we would soon find Father's East Stream and be carried in its flow. Until my aunt groaned again, and as I reached toward her with the wine, I saw that her milk-white eyes stared straight into the sun, that they no longer saw anything at all. She was no longer moving. I thought: this is death. Her heaving chest no longer heaved, the sweat dried on her skin. Her jaw hung open like a seared gourd. The bloated squid of her belly quivered with the motion of the boat. She was dead, and I shuddered and recoiled from her, this horrific corpse that stank like the sea. I thought of diving out and swimming away, but I was a poor swimmer and afraid. Was she only sleeping? What did I know of death? I shouted her name, then my name, which I had hours ago withheld, but she only stared into the sun with her milk-white eyes. I felt shamed, as if I had failed her. Perhaps there really was such a place as the Island of the Blessed, and my aunt had lost her chance to go there. I wiped the sweat from her face with the blanket and tried to spread it to cover her but it would not. I was stirred by my duty to her and determined to find the place where her body belonged, and resumed oaring on our current course, though I had no course. When the sun set and the temperature cooled I tired, as if the sun's heat had enlivened me and without it I was nothing. An awful fear again overtook me, and misery, and the mystery her death represented and my journey had failed to solve. My duty to her now paled compared to a growing panic that I would join her if I did not soon find my way. I considered dropping her anywhere—no one would know, but I would know, and my father would know, and the gods. How long could I go on oaring? Already I'd drunk a flagon of water, though the salt fish remained—underneath the head of my dead aunt. Night, and no moon, no stars, no way to distinguish sky from sea, so we seemed to float suspended in a great black chasm, and only the lapping of the waves recalled the existence of the waters. I tried to comfort myself with memories of home but found none I could recall, only the face of the Whistle Cliffs disappearing. A large fish knocked against the boat, and I sank into a restless sleep.

When I woke the sun was risen. I was lying with my head next to the stinking feet of my dead aunt. I jumped and crawled back into the stern. Her body had stiffened, become rigid, her arms reaching stupidly for the sky. At first I was frightened, then heard myself laugh out loud. So this is what we come to in the end! Frozen in our own fluids, like some comical fossil. Why, I said, I might tie her to a rope and drop her body into the sea like an anchor! I snatched the salt fish from under her head and ate eagerly, gulping the second flagon of water. This grotesque body, I decided, had nothing to do with my aunt Milori, and so it made no difference what I did with it. Besides, I might well have passed the East Stream long ago. Or perhaps

I was floating in it now. Or perhaps there was no East Stream, no more than an Island of the Blessed, my father slyly refuting one lie with a lie of his own. It seemed a thing he would do. And so I heaved the body of my aunt into the sea—she sank immediately—and began rowing in the direction I thought was east. But I was not sure if home was east, and oared on in hallucinatory wonderment at the impossibility of it all. I thought I saw my dead aunt beside me. I thought I saw my father on the horizon. I thought I heard my dead aunt's hisses from the bottom of the sea. I thought I saw a cliff shag diving into the sea, and emerging with a fish twisting, and flying away with it. I thought I saw another shag, and another, until I realized they must be real, these shags, and they would return with the fish to their nests on our island. And so I followed them, gaining strength with the cleverness of my plan, and hissing at the sea as it hissed back at me. By evening I could see the great face of the Whistle Cliffs, burning red, illuminated by the setting sun. But instead of rowing home, I waited. Was my father lost at sea? Or would I find him in the cottage? The idea of seeing him filled me with shame. I'd done Milori a terrible injustice. My father would know this, his own sister dumped into the rank black sea. I was sunburned badly, the muscles cramping in my arms and legs. I gulped the flagon of wine and lay frozen in drink and doubt. Again I slept fitfully, but woke in the morning surprised to hear voices—during the night my scow had washed ashore.

"No oarsman ever came home like this before."

"Just floated up out of nowhere."

"Asleep the whole time."

"What'll we do with two oarsmen?"

"Could mean a lot of dying."

Smalt and Bice, old fishermen, not too old to haul me roughly out of the scow, and my legs aching. They said Father had returned the day before, but no one had seen him since. I parted ways with them, who had no interest in hearing of my journey, and begged me to silence when I tried to describe it. I climbed the mossy shale to our cottage and found Father splitting logs. He didn't seem to see me, and I stood at the edge of the clearing and watched, as he stood each log on the stump, raised the axe wearily and held it above his head as if unsure what, now, he should do with it. Each time he seemed to bend lower, the weight too much for him, then he surprised me by the savage strength with which he struck. Sometimes he split the log, sometimes missed. Either way, he pushed it aside and began again. I entered the clearing and carried the wood to the pile, while he positioned another log and struck again. We carried on in silence, Father sweating, taking increasingly longer between blows. I burned to tell him of my travels, or to hear of his, but he remained quiet. Finally he sat on the stump, hands resting on his knees, his grotesque knuckles, hands bone white with chill though these sunny afternoons were the warmest of the year. He moved slowly, wary of me, or of unknown forces he sensed were conspiring against him. I thought of a life made of the kind of voyage that I'd struggled to complete just once—the toil he'd endured. And yet he never complained.

"There's no place out there except the sea," I said. "Is that true, Father?"

He pushed himself up from the stump, placed his cold hand on my face and smiled. "Could be," he said. "That could be."

"What about the East Stream?"

"You're the oarsman now," he said.

"But I don't know what I'm doing."

"Yes," he said, and he was laughing, and the wrinkles in ripples beside his eyes. "May I ask how is it you intend to learn?"

The next days Father rarely left the cottage. He maintained a genial distance, noting what of nature he'd observed: two new shag nests, a colony of jellyfish, the tide rising higher than it had in months. I argued with him in my mind for hours, rehearsing my own justifications, finding ways to blame him. Around the village I was regarded warily by the elders, who questioned my claim to the title of oarsman. I dreaded returning to the sea, but I heard of no one with the sickness, as if the villagers were preserving their health until the question of oarsman was resolved. By the youth I was treated with increasing respect, which I enjoyed, even as I feared the new responsibility. Occasionally a villager would give me a gift, or a gift for Father, but when I returned home I would not admit these gifts were intended for him, but only for me, and I would cry out, "See, Father! Look what Auramine gave me in the market!" Father pretended to take no notice but later I would discover a few slayberries or a pheasant egg gone missing. At first I believed he stole these to satisfy the pride he used to take in such things, or simply to treat himself to this small, secret indulgence. But later I realized he may have stolen them to remind me of my own thefts, and my dishonesty. As I watched him chop wood in the afternoons, I took guilty satisfaction in seeing him miss more frequently, and the pine piled roof high since he burned it less freely now, hoarding it. Nights he spent in bed, sleeping, shouting out hoarsely with nightmares by the fire.

And then one day I returned from fishing—I no longer hid this from him—and found him warming his hands in a steaming bowl of water, and the clouds milk white behind the pupils of his eyes.

"Father, your eyes."

"It's remarkable," he said. "I can see more clearly now," and he led me outside, and pointed to a shag nest, high in a cypress halfway down the mountain, and asked how many fledglings did I see. Cliff shags only nest in dead trees, the tree with its black branches leaned under the nest's weight. All these things I could see, but no fledglings, no birds at all. "Five!" he shouted, with the excitement of a child. "I can see five—four black, and one with white wings."

"That is extraordinary."

"And do you see the father, returning to its nest?" he asked.

"Yes," I lied—my eyes had never been as strong as his.

"Well, what does it have in its mouth?" he asked.

"A fish," I guessed.

"No—an eel!" he shouted, laughing, and I marveled, the sickness cripples everyone, but my father, it makes him stronger. But then he said he could see every detail of the eel, the yellow spots behind its gills, and the shag itself, afflicted with tiny parasites, missing two feathers underneath its wing.

That night when my father fell asleep, I barred the door to keep him inside, and climbed out the window. At Crale's cottage, I told him what had happened, and told him to prepare Father's bark as he had prepared my scow before, with water, food, and wine. I told him to tell no one, we would leave in an hour. Back at our cottage, Father tossed in bed, sweating. I held a candle above his eyes, hoping to see them cleared, but the film covered them entirely. "Let's go, Father," I said. "It's time for us to go." He had thrown off the sheets and lay sweating, though his body glowed bone white with cold. He peered at me down the long angle of his nose.

"Where?" he said.

"To the bark."

He looked at me, then looked away.

"It's Milori," I lied. "Her body's washed ashore."

"Milori?"

"Yes. It's my fault."

"What has this to do with me?"

"You must take her body back to sea, to release her properly."

"At night?"

"So the village will never know."

"On one condition."

"Yes?" I asked.

"You come with us," he said, and smiled at me mischievously. He rose from the bed, and reached for his clothes, remembering with his hands exactly where he'd left them. He needed no help descending the mountain in the dark, as if he remembered the location of each curve or boulder in the path. Only once did he stumble. "Getting darker," he said, and I took his elbow, and with shame and dread I led him on. A sliver of moon was visible through the clouds, and the phantom light fell on the bark and the pebbles of the beach. "I hear the waves," he said. "But where is my sister?"

"In the bark," I said.

"She's alive?"

"No."

"Good. I never could stand that woman."

Crale had prepared the bark with the water and wine, a sack of fish. Father felt for the gunwale and lowered himself into his seat, taking pleasure in feeling the oars in his hands. I thought he might be too weak to row, this was supposed to be my job after all. I'd lied to trick him down to the beach, but now resented having to tell that lie, and wanted to claim my rightful place behind the oars. But Father looked at me defiantly with his dry, colorless eyes. I shoved us off. "Now," he said, rowing, "where is this stinking corpse of Milori?" I said nothing. "You see it is not so easy to lie to your father." He oared us out to sea, and I turned back to see the looming shoulders of the Whistle Cliffs, glowing in the moonlight.

Finally I asked where we were going. "How should I know?" he said. "I am your passenger, as it were."

"No, I am yours."

"Oh? Yes, so it is. Well. We shall see."

"Father," I said with emotion, "you're making a mockery of me, and the duties of the oarsman."

"Not at all," he said and smiled.

It seemed Father would never tire, on and on for hours, with the same unbearable strength and rhythm, and the boat gliding across the sea like it was pulled across a block of ice. As long as he continued oaring, he was thinking, death would not touch him. I cursed his vanity, and pulled long drafts from the flagon of wine, glaring into his milky eyes, glowing in the dark. His will was relentless, but in the bark I saw proof of aging—his withered lips disappeared within his hoary beard, bone-white hands clutching the oars. I yearned for his death, and feared what his death would bring. He began taunting me, asking where were we, and how would I find my way back home. He didn't know how I'd followed the shags, but I didn't know whether the trick would work again, whether they ventured this far. Father claimed mischievously that we had arrived in another realm. The path, he said, is written on the white-capped pattern of the waves. The moon had disappeared, and in the black night I searched the horizon for signs of the rising sun. Had Father oared us into the world to come? I gulped large drafts from the flagon. Father sang fishing chanties at the top of his lungs. I told myself he had little time left to live. Father whistled and called out greetings to the gods. I vomited over the gunwale. Father laughed and told me to sit up, open my eyes. I fell asleep as Father rowed on.

That was not the last I saw of him, but it seemed it might be, when I woke and the sun was shining and Father was gone. He always told me we remember everything that ever happened to us, nothing in our minds is lost. He claimed I could remember the death of my mother, if I wasn't afraid of trying. He claimed to remember every meal, every moment he'd spent with every man and woman he had oared to sea. And I would try to remember such things, I would try, as he said, to be unafraid, and recall the awful memories as well as the good. But here was something else at which I failed. I have no memory of Mother's death. I remember little from childhood, good or bad, but I know now the reason is not because I'm afraid, but because I don't need to remember. I'm content in the present and have no need of the past. And I know Father tried to observe every detail of every moment, and committed these moments to memory, because he wanted to preserve them like fossils, forever. The villagers knew him as the instrument of change, but I knew him as a man afraid of change, and I knew when I found him gone from the boat that he loved me as his son but resented the change I was meant to bring, and he accused me of fearing the past to hide his fears of the future.

But it's not true I have forgotten the past, I remember parts of it well. I remember smiling to find, with the sunrise, that the shags did venture this far, we were not in another realm after all, and I followed them home as before, their beaks full for the young to feed. I remember a giant fish leaping writhing into the air and falling back helplessly into the sea. I remember arriving within sight of the island at dusk, waiting until the dark, and oaring ashore. I hid the bark among the trees, seeing no need for it anymore. And, in time, the villagers would agree, for the next morning they found my father, beaten but breathing, strewn with seaweed, having swum all day and night and collapsed on the beach. Crale and I carried him up the shale to my cottage, blind, bone white and silent. His cold skin stank and came away in our hands. He died soon after, lying in his bed, and a fire blazing beside him. The villagers begged me to carry his body away and release it to sea, perhaps the gods would not take notice. But I said nothing escapes the gods' notice, just as nothing escaped my father's. Only unlike my father's, the gods' observation carried with it no judgment, we were free to do as we pleased, and so I burned my father's corpse in the clearing behind our cottage. His bones I buried in the clearing, and I piled the earth high on top of the bones. The villagers hid in their homes, waiting for divine retribution, an outbreak of disease, a wave that would swallow us all. But nothing happened, and some villagers began venturing out, until a few days later Milori's body washed ashore, and again they grew terrified. But again nothing happened, and though I felt more sure now in my convictions, still I wondered if my father perhaps had known of some secret place after all, else why had Milori returned, and none before? But I told myself it didn't matter whether her body rested here or at the bottom of the sea, and I burned it as I did my father's, and buried her bones next to his. The villagers began to venture out for good. Some said when my father died on the island the gods died, too, and we were alone now with nothing to save us. Some said the gods would live as long as we believed in them, it was our faith that fed them, as sunlight feeds the trees. And some said the gods still lived, but their wrath would not be visited on us but on the dead, whose souls would not find comfort until they found the sea. But I stood among them and said it was all absurd, and I told them death was a great mystery. I invited them out beyond the horizon, to explore the unknown sea for themselves. But no one listened to what I said, and no one listens to me now, and they do not give me any gifts, but openly despise me. For I am no longer the oarsman, and in truth I never was.

THE MARKET

Leah Swanson thought: formliness is in the eye of the beholder—well, let them behold. She was wearing chandelier earrings and a slinky cashmere dress with a ruched waist in flight jacket green, which was unlike any other color worn at the market by any other girl. She'd refused all her mother's suggestions not because her mother was wrong but because Leah liked being stubborn. She waited with the other bluebells on benches under the awning as the men made their bids. Anthony Cantwell was almost half a foot taller than his friends. Leah could see him standing at the back of the crowd, laughing, showing that cockeyed grin that made him look pleasantly drunk. She liked to play with his name. Canthony Antwell. Antcant Wellthony. Antwellthony. A week before the market, she sent him a note: *Let me go ahead and apologize for my quiet Saturday. I was too busy getting depressed again but I guess you understand. By the way—are you sure it was just allergies? Because now I've got your runny nose. Not that I care. I finally got to try on a couple of Dawn Gibbons's formal dresses but Mom says I can't wear them because Dawn is a slut.* Anthony didn't write back but that was because before he got the chance, they saw each other at Katy's formal. He said that Dawn couldn't be a slut since she sold last year as a capital bride. Leah said, "What's the difference between a capital bride and a slut anyway? I don't think I even know anymore." Then Anthony said, "Capital brides are expensive. Sluts you get for cheap," which cracked her up—classic Anthony. From her bench, she could see his head but not his feet—she wondered if he was wearing the furry slippers. His friends accused him of wearing the furry slippers to get attention but actually it was because his feet got cold.

This past week took the cake for worst dressed. She broke her record and was revolting four days in a row. Of course having Anthony's cold didn't help—her eyes were watery and her nose was running and anyway, her dossier was finished, so when it came to impressing her teachers, what was the point? Her mother tried to insist on what she wore to school but that only provoked Leah to wear something else. On her last day she wore the turquoise earrings with the circus vest and cowboy belt. Needless to say, when she walked into class, she had everybody staring. It was great. She did get scolded because she didn't have a positive mental attitude on her last day—which wasn't fair because she was actually trying to behave. She even made up with Maggie Woodat and told her that she hoped Aaron Sanders bought her, even though everybody knew that Aaron was going to buy Janet Arline. She had to sit in the bleachers on the last day of school with the rest of the class and watch as her friends Melissa and Anne Marie demonstrated how you were supposed to climb the steps onto the stage, and how you were supposed to stand while the Auctioneer described your assets, and how you were supposed to smile and how you were supposed to turn. The last thing that Mrs. Belenky said to her was better brush your hair for the market and put on lipstick, and of course Leah fell out laughing. She detested Mrs. Belenky, who taught maternity, but really liked Mrs. Watson, who taught civics. She actually hated civics, but she loved Mrs. Watson's sarcasm and her goofy sense of humor.

Now all the widows were knocked down and the Auctioneer was finally moving on to the bluebells. She missed exchanging snarky comments with Melissa and Anne Marie—they split you up so you couldn't be with your friends. Sitting to her immediate right was Victoria Smith, who reeked of cigarettes. Leah and Victoria hadn't been on speaking terms since Victoria told Sam what Leah wrote about him in the Seedling. Anne Marie was in the front row and Melissa was three rows back. Anne Marie had been a charm bunny for the past month trying to get a better behavior grade in her dossier since she got Bs in maternity and poetry. She got an A in algebra for which she was overly proud. Leah got a B+ in algebra even though she was better at math than anyone in the class. But they all got higher grades because they cheated on the final exam.

Sitting to her immediate left was an intriguing girl from Western that Leah knew only by reputation—Ameline Seward. With her piercing eyes and cutting dimples and catalog form, Ameline was a sure bet for a capital bride except for her terrible attitude. She was famous for telling Bradley Dufour at the civic awards ceremony that she felt sorry for him, and when Bradley asked why, she said, "Because sobriety is hard. Yet you've been sober two hours straight." And she'd caused a sensation a week ago when, unlike every other blue-bell ever, she'd refused to take a turn with Glassen's mayor in the hot-air balloon. Leah introduced herself, asked Ameline's name, pretending she didn't know her.

"Am-e-line," said Ameline, pronouncing each syllable distinctly as if to compensate for her slight lisp. "Rhymes with *gasoline*."

"I like your dress," said Leah, which was the only nice thing she could think to say. Actually Ameline looked peculiar. Leah appreciated an idiosyncratic wardrobe but only if it enhanced your appearance whereas, with Ameline's outfit, it was like she'd deliberately made herself unattractive. Her sleeves were bunched at the shoulders and her cheeks were pale and powdery as if brushed with chalk. And her hair was strange—unruly but in a packaged way, like one of those wreaths made out of plastic leaves. "Is that silk charmeuse?"

Ameline laughed—a fizzy, vigorous laugh that exposed her large teeth and gums. "That's perfect. Of course you like the dress. Because it's Mother's. Everyone always likes it when it's Mother's."

"I've always been lousy at compliments."

"I didn't mean it that way. What you said was sweet," said Ameline, and she touched Leah on the wrist.

"I just wish this was over," said Leah.

"God, me too," said Ameline. Always she was wrestling her body into some sort of contortion—now she crossed then uncrossed her legs, cast her feet wide, placed them at an extreme inward angle. "Have you ever thought we should get married by lottery? It'd be just as random, but we could skip the bidding and all the other nonsense."

"No matter how you do it," said Leah, "there's going to be nonsense. So long as boys are involved. Not that I care. I just leave it all up to the invisible hand."

For some reason Ameline found this funny and laughed—a frothy, undignified laugh that could cost a girl dollars on the line. "Oh sure—the invisible hand!" she said. "Does the market have an invisible foot, too? Invisible stomach? Invisible mustache?"

That cracked Leah up—she couldn't help it, she had to laugh, she had to pinch herself and think of her poor dead dog, Rupert, to stop laughing before she attracted attention. She'd never heard a girl make fun of the invisible hand before. It wasn't the kind of thing you were supposed to do if you were trying to have a positive mental attitude. The invisible hand was the agent of a girl's salvation. The invisible hand determines a price for every girl and distributes every girl to the man who's meant to be her husband. That's what they taught in home economics anyhow. She got a B+ in home ec because her soufflé fell.

Among the many young men in attendance there were a few older bachelors, ranging from wealthy widowers like councilman Julius Calash to aspirants from the burgeoning middle class, men like Clay Gainous, who sold sewing machines out of a shop on Crawford. After years in the trade, Gainous had acquired some means and his gains were attributable not to salesmanship or charm but perseverance and skill—he had a talent for moving parts. His short black hair was balding but unlike many who suffered from a similar embarrassment he made no effort to conceal it. Small, orderly teeth, a rounded nose that gave off a glare, and the darkling apparition of bristle about his jaw that never went away no matter how closely he shaved.

Gainous had begun attending the market five years ago. With the garment-makers contract, his business was showing promise: the time had come to buy a wife. To calculate how much he could afford, he considered the current state of his affairs and possible scenarios for the future: pessimistic, cautiously optimistic, optimistic. The price of cotton could spike, which might send the garment makers south, ending his most lucrative contracts. But if cotton stabilized or if the new treadle models increased output by a third (as was claimed) or even by a fifth (as might reasonably be expected)—well, he could become a rich man. He regarded the prospect of mediocrity with sobriety, likewise the prospect of wealth.

At his first market, he came prepared to spend a predetermined amount based on conservative estimates of his likely wealth, with a thorough knowledge of the girls available in his price range, but he was dismayed to find that as soon as he bid another bid rushed in, as if his bid never existed. He offered another bid but it was immediately overtaken. The bids crashed like waves all about him: like some floundering ocean swimmer, he could hardly find his footing. His careful analysis of the assets of this girl over that, his charts and tables, were scattered like debris on the tide. Arthur Fux (rhymes with *dukes*) was a surveyor who had appraised three new developments in the wiregrass and opened his own office with a storefront on Broad, he spent thrice on his wife what Gainous had planned to spend. Gainous overheard him say, "I don't care what she cost. Only eight capital brides this year and by God, I got one of them." Gainous saw that the girls he thought he desired were not the girls that were desired by the men he wished to emulate.

At the market two years later, he was a man of means: the price of cotton had stabilized, and he came to the market at Glassen prepared to purchase a capital bride who met the approval of Arthur Fux and other men whose accomplishments he admired. He had braced himself to compete with the frenzy of bids, to throw himself in that rough water, understanding that all courtship is competition and that wealth is only one measure of success; the rest is what you do with it. And so he bid on Ruth Jefferson and Julia Sullivan, Ashley Adams and Christy Marshall, all on the Club's list of likely capital brides. He bid with quiet determination undeterred by the bids of others but in the end he couldn't close the deal. He was a failure: what kind, he wasn't sure. The girls had many assets: straight teeth, narrow noses, radiant skin. They were formly. But their formliness was ordinary. He wanted the best that money could buy, yet no girl seemed superior to any other. When he looked into their faces, he felt no fear that he might on her behalf commit some grievous error. He was no romantic but he wanted to get what he paid for.

When Leah had refused to dress appropriately the last week of school, her mother criticized her for having a negative mental attitude. Her father didn't care about her attitude, he only cared that she sold for enough money that she wasn't an embarrassment. He threatened that she'd wind up in the pitchhole but they both knew it wasn't true. Only disfigured girls wound up in the pitchhole, like Emma Graham who was born without a hand, or the mute girls, or the sluts who got knocked up. Leah had no idea what she'd go for. Some nights she woke sweating, throwing up, fearing the worst. Other times, she told herself it didn't matter—it was out of her hands—the market would take care of it. There was no sentimental bullshit with the market—that's what she liked about it. There was no reason to get excited just like there was no reason to get depressed. Some girls got silly with romantic longing like Anne Marie who carried around a dollar bill in a locket from Daniel Hanson, who promised to buy her. Anthony Cantwell didn't make promises and that's why Leah liked him. He was a realist. He said he didn't know what would happen at the market, it all came down to the invisible hand. She didn't care how much she sold for as long as it was more than Jessica Beckett. Jessica who ate hamburgers every night for dinner while binging laxatives and bragging about her twenty-eight-inch waist. Jessica who kissed Anthony at the spring dance.

Now being auctioned was a girl Leah knew from Eastern, Susan Kean. They played on the tennis team together. Susan was number three singles whereas Leah was demoted to junior varsity because her serve went into a permanent funk. Susan was the only girl Leah had ever seen hit a one-handed backhand like a boy. She couldn't hit it with any velocity but she sliced with so much backspin it gave her opponents fits. She was plain faced, but the Auctioneer ignored that, calling attention instead to her "motherly" measurements, as well as her career 3.9 GPA and composite behavior score of 92, including high marks for patience and flexibility. He didn't say anything about her one-handed backhand. Three years ago, Leah had to sing a duet with Susan, and Susan couldn't remember the words so they had to start over, then Leah couldn't quit laughing, then Susan started laughing and they never finished the duet. Now Susan was laughing nervously as the Auctioneer joked, "Her brain's solid as a walnut, no cracks," and he gave her skull a knock—"See, I just checked it." She sold at twenty-three fifty, and the brass band played a celebratory tune.

A couple of girls took ordinary turns onstage, then poor Cressy Foster, who had palsy. She stood refusing to face the audience with her back to the crowd wearing a dress with the color and texture of wet bark. The Auctioneer started her bids in the pitchhole. "Now who will take eight hundred dollars for this agreeable girl with weak legs but good teeth?"

"Is that for her backside or do I get the front too?"

"Eight hundred, now seven seventy-five, all right, thank you, Luther, who'll take seven fifty?" As the bids continued to drop, Cressy began to lean, her right leg shook, it looked as if any moment she might fall, provoking the Auctioneer hastily to put an end to the bidding. "Sold to Luther Bloom at six thirty-five!"

"When do I get my cash?" said Bloom.

"Half now," said the Auctioneer, taking Cressy by the arm and helping her down the steps. "Half after a month when you give her a good home."

And the brass band played a celebratory tune.

Then Jessica Beckett, who wasn't wearing a dress but a maxiskirt, probably because she thought it elongated her legs, but she got the top all wrong. She could play the fiddle except she called it the violin because she was a snob. She played a ridiculous little screechy tune while the men started bidding and there was Anthony Cantwell stepping forward with his cockeyed grin and yes he was wearing the furry slippers and he was jacking up his stick bidding a thousand. He was laughing about it with Doug and Lex so he was just joking around. He was always joking around. He liked to give everything jokey names. He called his father Mr. Orangutan and he named his car the Blue Pineapple. He even named the lawnmower—it was called Adolphus. Sometimes he called Leah Pookie and sometimes he called her Sassafras which he rhymed with *sweet ass*. Now Jessica wasn't playing the fiddle, she was strutting back and forth in front of the Auctioneer in a jerky, propulsive way as if she were being prodded with a stick. Anthony bid twenty-two hundred and he was no longer laughing. They told her that, to maintain a positive mental attitude, she needed to look for the good in people, find alternative explanations, give people the benefit of the doubt. She tried to give Anthony the benefit of the doubt. He's just trying out his process, she thought. He wants to see what it feels like to bid on a girl. Except if he was just trying out his process, how come he kept bidding? Didn't he know that Jessica had a 100 percent fake laugh? That she cheated on her algebra exam? That she had that weird smell when it rained? Boys were encouraged to bid on a variety of girls, even girls that weren't a high priority. She'd heard it so often it was annoying: a boy never knows what he thinks about a girl until he bids her. Competition from other men might excite a man to frenzy over a girl never noticed or dissolve the desire for a girl long admired into nothing. That was the wisdom of the invisible hand. But what if the invisible hand informed Anthony that he belonged with Jessica Beckett? And why had Anthony just bid three thousand, which was a lot of money for the son of a banker who joked that he was broke? In the end it was Brian Jordan who won Jessica, not Anthony Cantwell, at a capital price of fifty-one hundred, but that didn't make her feel any better. I don't need him anyhow—look at all these bachelors with more class, you could tell because they wore real shoes to get married not furry slippers, which Anthony was wearing like the clown that he was.

Then came the foreign girl. She'd only been in town three weeks but everybody knew about her. She was from one of those frozen tundra countries with unpronounceable names. Unlike the other girls, she wore her hair unembellished, no plaits, no bangs, no curls, only the icy-blond hair long and elegant like the drape of a veil and the peculiar way she placed her nimble feet as she walked. Leah was surprised by how old she looked—the Auctioneer claimed she was nineteen, but any idiot could see she was at least twenty-three. The Auctioneer's attention lit up her face as the sun lights up the moon; there was something haunting to her luster.

"Now here's a young lady with a felicity for tongues," said the Auctioneer. "I don't mean your tongues, I mean languages: she speaks a half dozen. She even speaks English, go ahead, sweetheart, tell them your hobby."

"I like to dancing," she said. Her lips moved a little shape-lessly when she talked; dimples formed not in her cheeks but chin. She wore no footwear: her feet, perfectly formed, would be disfigured by something so crude as a pair of shoes.

"Her name's Nadezhda," said the Auctioneer. "Now isn't she formly?"

The bachelors were intrigued. They looked her up and down and crowded closer to get a better view. But not every-one was pleased. A gaunt man with a haggard beard named Mr. Whitish shouted over the crowd, "I've never seen such outrageousness!" He had a harried expression, hands that shook. To eliminate unpleasant incidents, parents weren't allowed at market until after their daughters had been sold. Mr. Whitish had shown up shortly after his daughter Hannah had been knocked down for a disappointing sum.

"She is remarkable," said the Auctioneer, "isn't she, Mr. Whitish?"

"The market's no place for foreign girls," said Whitish. "Put her back on the boat!"

"Boat?" said the Auctioneer. "We're five hundred miles from the nearest coast!"

"Just get her out of here," said Whitish. Even at some distance you could see red streaks on his neck from the morning shave.

"Now what good would that do?" said the Auctioneer jovially. "The market wants every girl it can get. Variety's better for everybody."

"Bullshit!" shouted Whitish. "The market don't want a goddamn thing."

"We're the market!" shouted a bachelor from the back. "And we want Nadezhda!" And the crowd erupted into catcalls.

"Sore loser!"

"Too much booze!"

They were accustomed to the dismay of fathers disappointed by their daughter's bride prices but making accusations was poor sportsmanship. The marriage of girls isn't charity. If you want comfort for your daughter, buy her a teddy bear. As Sheriff Chesson escorted Mr. Whitish from the festivities, Nadezhda seemed unconcerned by the disturbance. Maybe she didn't understand what exactly had happened, thought Leah. Maybe she was accustomed to outbursts of anger. Maybe she believed that she needn't concern herself with such trash.

"Poor thing," Ameline said to Leah. "All alone in a foreign land."

"Poor thing?" said Leah. "She's going to be a capital bride. Not bad for a girl who doesn't use deodorant."

"Pardon?" said Ameline.

"Foreign girls don't use deodorant. That's what Anthony says anyway. Probably just another one of his gags."

"She seems to know how to use a tube of lipstick, though," said Ameline.

All right gentlemen, this girl's going to cost you if you want her, now who wants her? Three thousand, three thousand if you want to dance, this ain't no flapjack this is the continental waltz.

"I bet she knows more English than she lets on," said Leah. "She's just pretending so she doesn't have to say anything. I wish I could get away with something like that. My life would be better if I didn't have to respond to every little thing that idiot boys said."

"You say that," said Ameline, "but you don't actually believe it."

"What do you mean?"

"I mean you take a negative view of everything but here you are, perfect little market bride," said Ameline. Her hands were wound tightly together—she was a repository of energy, like the twisted rope of a catapult. "You've got the right dress and the right earrings and you're sitting exactly the right way they want you to sit."

Forty-five hundred to Ed Alford, I need fifty, fifty if you want her. Where are you, Donald? How about you, Mike? We're not wasting time with chicken feeders, give me your best or get lost, she's a looker and a thinker, I'm at fifty, now fifty-four, fifty, fifty, fifty, fifty-four hundred to Donald, where are you, Rich?

It was not surprising that Ameline wasn't fooled by Leah's attempts to project a positive mental attitude. And it was irritating that she hadn't noticed Leah's dress—that it was different from everyone else's. Nobody wore flight jacket green because supposedly it robbed your skin of color—Leah wore it anyway but Ameline didn't care about that. It was easy to ignore fashion if you were formly like Ameline. "I'm actually very independent," said Leah. "You will be happy to know that I got a B in poetry because Ms. Ballard said my explication was weird and totally different from the norm."

Ameline let out an explosive, toothy laugh. "That'll show them! And did you go on a hunger strike at lunch and refuse to eat your blueberry cheesecake?"

Mike at sixty-six, now eight, now eight, I want a sixty-eight-hundred-dollar bid, watch how she runs those fingers through her hair, gentlemen, watch how her hair shimmers in the sunshine as it falls from those formly hands, thank you mister, sixty-eight to the handsome stranger with the Vandyke beard, now who'll give me seventy, formliest girl in the wiregrass, I'm at seventy, seventy, seventy, you're slowing down when you should be speeding up.

"Well but I mean, what's a girl supposed to do?" said Leah. "I have to get married—nothing will change that. Might as well let the market make the arrangement—it's as good as anything else they've tried."

Ameline scoffed, gave Leah a sardonic glare. Her lips painted garishly red gave her complexion a peppermint gleam.

"Wait, you're not one of those sappy romantics, are you?" said Leah. "Passionate kisses? Strawberries and cream? Long sighs and feverish letters and unrequited love—all that?"

"No, I'm no fool—of course not. Boys aren't worth it. But also—this is *my* life. You know? Not Mother's. Not theirs."

Watch her prop her hands on those hips and pout when she thinks she's been insulted, listen to her coo at you come daybreak like the mew of a mourning dove, they call her Nadezhda and let me tell you she's got the formliest hands this side of the great divide.

"At least the market's natural," said Leah. "I guess it's Darwinian, if you think about it."

"You mean natural like animals are natural?" said Ameline. "Like lions and gorillas in the jungle? Because I thought we're not animals, we're human."

Leah didn't have an answer for that. If Ameline couldn't see the difference between gorillas breaking each other's necks to win a mate and an auction guided by the invisible hand, then there was no hope for her. The market connected the formliest girls with the richest men—that made sense. And it connected mediocre girls with mediocre men—and so on down the line. It wasn't romantic but life wasn't a romance so might as well get on with it. She felt the afternoon sun cutting in under the awning, scorching the tip of her nose. She wished she'd put on more sunscreen.

What an auction! Does it end now or does Mike have it in him for one more bid? Now wait a minute, here comes another bidder, thank you, Mr. Cantwell, that's Anthony Cantwell with an eight-thousand-dollar bid, eighty-five, eighty-five, I've got an eight-thousand-dollar bid from Mr. Cantwell in the bedroom slippers and old-fashioned frock coat, eighty-five hundred, thank you, Vandyke, can I get ninety ninety ninety, that's nine triple zero, thank you, Mr. Cantwell, he's got a hot heart but cold feet, ninety-five, ninety-five hundred if you want her. Let me tell you she knows how to move a room. She's elegant, she's exotic, nine-thousand-dollar bid, now nine, give me ninety-five, I want you to look at that face, this is a girl smart and marvelous. Nadezhda going once! Nadezhda going twice! Nadezhda sold to Anthony Cantwell in the bedroom slippers for nine thousand dollars!

Some grooms dislike a hot market, thought Clay Gainous. They're driven to bid and win on the first formly girl who comes along just to get out of the heat. But Gainous knew the heat makes choosing a bride easier: when the sun climbs above the longleaf pines and the breeze dies off the Porry and the hot air reels with humidity, some girls wilt right off, their color sours and their bangs collapse and they lose the energy even to fan themselves. Formly girls, smart girls, large girls—no matter their virtues, if a girl can't stand the heat, she's not worth a wooden nickel.

This was Gainous's first market in years. Unlike last time he had no interest in scouting the field, no interest in throwing himself helplessly among a welter of bids. He was here to buy one girl and one girl only—and he was pleased to see that, unlike so many of her peers, she took no notice of the heat but sat still with her back erect, gaining strength as the day wore on.

One night four months ago, at a performance of the Roberts Amusement Co., something went wrong with the cannonball fired at the buffalo and the buffalo went down. Gainous knew what happened to wounded animals and approached the ringmaster with an offer. For a price, Roberts hauled the animal, lying on its side and not moving but for the rise and fall of its bellowing lungs, to Gainous's home. A vet was called, who set the bones and said, "Clay Gainous, you got the world beat now, don't you?" There was hay for feed and cornmeal and lard and the buffalo ate it all. Gainous lived on a corner lot with a tricornered backyard in the middle of which was the buffalo. One day the buffalo was not lying but standing, bluebirds picking at its mane. The ag regulator said, "There's no law says you can't keep her, but no law says you can, either." Gainous named her Beulah and removed the splint from the bone. A week later he came home and Beulah was standing in the front rather than the back. The fence was closed. He led Beulah back inside the gate and the next day found her in someone else's yard. A terrified neighbor said he saw the buffalo leap the fence—it came from nowhere, said his neighbor, this hurtling mass, like a sofa thrown from a window. The ag man returned and called Beulah a menace. In one week the sheriff would shoot her unless Gainous found her a proper home. He called the Quadruped Committee and the Barn League but it was no use. He was moved by the quiet majesty of the beast and by the superior greatness of the greatest things. The day before the sheriff's arrival he decided to shoot Beulah himself but returned with his uncle's gun to find her gone. The neighbor said she leapt the fence and kept going, she trampled Ms. Garth's rose beds and hooked her horns on the white wash drying on the line. Gainous did not regard Beulah's departure as evidence of her ingratitude but foreknowledge of her doom, and he knew what it took the ag man three weeks to confirm: the buffalo would not be found. Mourning her loss, he wept: his need for a companion was exposed, and, too, the irregular nature of his tastes, which could not be fashioned, as he had assumed, by the standards of others. Money would be his means for buying a wife but it would not be his guide.

He'd seen Leah Swanson at the grocery store and endeavored to discover everything he could about her. Her father was an anesthesiologist, her mother was the president of the Benevolent Society, whose tireless work made the new municipal theater possible with performances from regional celebrities—first building constructed downtown in the four decades since the War. But this was more information than he required. Because he had found her: a girl with formliness fit for the stage, elegant limbs and prodigal blond-brown hair. Her eyes suggested some arcane erotic knowledge. This girl who assured him of his sexual nature, this girl he would purchase as his own.

"Number twenty-six!" called the Auctioneer, and Leah gave a little gasp but didn't move. The Auctioneer called out twenty-six again and when no girl emerged, he flipped through his cards until he found her. "Leah Swanson! Is Leah here today?" And he attempted to peer at the girls under the awning, but the sun got into his eyes and he couldn't see a thing.

Still Leah didn't move. She felt a spasm in her leg, felt her lips contorting into a hideous grin. Why had Anthony Cantwell bought the foreign girl when only three days ago he said that foreign girls didn't use deodorant? And he said they were nasty and didn't shave their armpits. Then he paid nine thousand for Nadezhda from the tundra, which must be some kind of record.

Two spotters roamed the crowd to locate bids and now they sauntered over. They didn't know what Leah looked like so they peered over the girls' heads, waiting for a sign.

"Leah!" called the Auctioneer. He had an oblong head tilted off-kilter. "I'm calling. The market's calling. The invisible hand of God wants to pair you with the man of your dreams, I see him standing there lonesome for a bride."

Ameline touched her wrist. "It's you."

"I already know that!" hissed Leah. How it could all change in an instant. How you told yourself one thing but believed something else. But the thing you actually believed wasn't the thing you wanted to believe. She liked the market because it wasn't sentimental, because it subjected the foolishness of romance to the laws of economics. But then here comes the invisible hand like some psychotic fairy godmother, waving a magic wand, inspiring love in a boy where before there'd been only ridicule or even disgust. She felt like she'd been cheated out of something that she hadn't been promised but had certainly earned.

The spotters noticed Leah and Ameline, one pointed and the other made his way down the aisle. The brim of his cowboy hat was bent; when he drew close, he said, "No trouble now."

"It's me," said Ameline, "I'll go," and she stood to follow the spotter down the aisle. Onstage, she whispered to the Auctioneer, told him her number, described what had happened to Leah. "Thank you, Ameline," he said, "and God bless. We have Ameline Seward who has come in Leah's place to give her friend a little more time." Now he drew out his cards, he skipped through them until he found Ameline and declared, "Yessir, Ameline Seward," reading from her card, "a dreamland lively who enjoys playing the piano—her rendition of the Pluvius sonata won first prize!"

"You're making me sound more gifted than I am," said Ameline with her subtle lisp. Her silk dress was bunched about her waist and twisted at the shoulders like a pillowcase yanked on crooked. "Actually that's the only thing I can play on the piano. Been practicing the same sonata for a dozen years."

"See, that's what it says plain as day in her dossier," said the Auctioneer. "Extremely talented young lady though modest to a fault."

"You know what it doesn't say in my dossier?" said

Ameline. "That I detest children. And I have halitosis in the morning. And weird feet. Also, there's this." And she stepped toward the edge of the stage, crossed her legs giving her hips a dramatic twist, and with two fingers plucked the hair like a wreath of plastic leaves from her head, held the wig high and away from her, flung it onto the men below.

No one moved. Speechless, the Auctioneer stared. The crowd stared. Leah stared. She'd never seen a girl without hair before. Ameline's bald head was black and stubbled as a burnt field. Without her hair her eyes were gigantic; her dark eyebrows looked raw and unseemly as a thread stitching a wound.

"I'm just letting the boys know what I look like *exactly*," said Ameline. "Because buying a bride is difficult, if you're a boy. Boys should know what they're buying without a girl's hair getting in the way. The baldest girl in the wiregrass—just look at my formly scalp, free of lice and mange."

Her sarcasm was nearly as shocking to Leah as her hairlessness. Girls didn't talk like that—not to the Auctioneer, not to anyone.

The Auctioneer held his head unnaturally still while his fallen eyes cast glances at the stage, the crowd—at anyone other than Ameline. Finally he placed his hand over his chest as if pledging allegiance. "It pains me to see a girl ruin her God-given assets and for what?"

"Let's get this over with, shall we?" said Ameline.

"Ms. Ameline Seward, ladies and gentlemen," said the Auctioneer, and he started her bidding at a pitchhole five hundred, then five fifty, then six hundred to anyone who would take her. A half-blind girl with a country smell and dirt under her nails—a man would marry her if she could cook and sew. But a girl that's lost her mind? A girl like that's no good to anybody.

Leah watched as Ameline was knocked down in the pitchhole to Rodney Gambaro, who had a hard, slick hull of hair like a saddle, just released from jail for felony assault. It made no sense what Ameline had said: *This is my life.* If it ever was her life, it wasn't her life anymore. Her life belonged to Rodney Gambaro and she'd be lucky to survive five years. It was impossible not to admire her courage. Except courage in a girl had no market value.

Now it was Leah's turn—there was no avoiding it. But Ameline's boldness had dulled the sting of Anthony's betrayal. For years her teachers had compelled her to have a positive mental attitude, which was like trying to force a caterpillar to smile. How to describe Ameline's mental attitude? Not positive but powerful. Leah took her place onstage but closed her eyes. How was it that you could shut your eyes without effort and your mouth too but closing your ears was impossible? She didn't have to watch but she had to listen.

She heard the Auctioneer say, "All right, gentlemen, this is Leah Swanson, daughter of Christopher Swanson, the doctor, and Geraldine Swanson, philanthropist extraordinaire."

She heard an elderly lady say, "Kind of crowded, isn't it?"

And she heard a bird chirping incessantly, the same chirp over and over.

And she heard the Auctioneer summarize her assets and hit the highlights from her dossier.

And she heard, "I don't know how I lost all that money. Just bad luck I guess."

And she heard a dog whimpering and a man say, "Don't give it, she already got some."

And she heard the Auctioneer navigate the escalating bids, fifteen hundred, eighteen, two thousand.

And she heard someone shout, "That's not a bid, that's a scratch!"

And she heard, "Where's a fellow like me supposed to get that kind of money?"

And she heard the Auctioneer declare, "Hurrah, ladies and gentlemen, we've got a new bidder, Clay Gainous, Clay Gainous at two thousand, if they won't let him keep that buffalo, he'll buy a wife instead."

And she thought, Is this actually the only way to marry a girl? Maybe Ameline's right—why not a lottery? The epitome of antisentimentality. The market was supposed to make sure everyone got what they deserved, but instead the girls were fakes and the boys were idiots who didn't know how to calculate value just like no one cared that she was the only bluebell who didn't cheat on the algebra exam.

And she heard, "Twenty-seven hundred to Clay Gainous, now I want twenty-eight, twenty-eight to the gentleman in the turtleneck sweater, I want thirty, don't quit on me now, Martin, your judgment's right, we're just quibbling on the figures. Anybody else thinking about her at three thousand?

Are you done, Martin? Done, Ed? Clay Gainous bids three thousand."

And she heard the roar of an automobile and she heard, "Just because the law says it's legal don't mean it's not a crime."

And she heard, "Clay Gainous makes up his mind, no buffalo he wants a bride."

And she heard the brass band play a celebratory tune.

THE TOWER

The tower's height—the source among our scholars of end-less supposition—is the greatest of its marvels. Though the scholars' calculations are highly sophisticated, they must be substantiated by conjectures from history: We as a people have been climbing the tower, at a minimum, for the past 236 years, which is when the first records were begun. In that time we have undertaken 80 ascents in which we climbed a total of 642 floors. Since each floor is 9 feet, we have ascended in that time a total of 5,778 feet. Most scholars agree that the evidence indicates that our people lived in the tower for at least four or five decades prior to the first recordkeeping, while some scholars argue for more, a long prehistory of peoples climbing for generations with no reckoning of their elevation or distance from the golden plain.

To figure the height of our tower, one must know not only how high we've climbed but how much farther we have to go, and here we have more debate. Some argue that our arrival will come soon, that with only four or five more ascents we will reach the pinnacle and the sovereign will step from the throne onto the golden plain. And following the sovereign, the retinue will climb from the tower to the plain, then the regents, then the scholars, then the marshals, then the men, the gardeners and boilers and haulers and potters and shoemakers and beekeepers and stockkeepers, then the women and children, and the great race of civilization will climb in one long unending line up the stairs to the plain, leaving behind our dens of darkness and hovels. It is always inspiring to hear such talk—but we must remind ourselves to be sensible and pay heed to the more conservative scholars who argue, drawing persuasively on formulas having to do with the shadow cast by the tower on the cloudscape and the changing trajectory of the sun, that we have another three hundred floors to ascend or more and that it will not be us but our descendants who step from the tower onto the plain.

These predictions can be sobering, and some have begun questioning why it should be our descendants and not we ourselves who are the first to enjoy the rewards of the golden plain. Why, many have asked, does the sovereign limit us to climbing only a few floors on each ascent? And why don't we climb more frequently? We have averaged throughout our written history only about eight floors for each ascent, which occurs, on average, only approximately every three years. Not everyone climbs eight floors—only the most fortunate. Most are directed to climb less—in some cases, only a single floor. Children and the elderly have difficulty with the more ambitious climbs; so do fathers, struggling to carry all their family's provisions in a single trip, which is all that is permitted—it wouldn't do on such a momentous and topsy-turvy day to have everyone scurrying up and down the stairs, increasing the confusion a hundredfold. Even so, many believe that our people could manage more than eight floors for each ascent. Our strong young men who do not yet have families of their own could carry the elderly and the children up the stairs. And our ascent could be extended beyond a single day—if properly organized—to a period of days or weeks. Our legends tell of a time when our people, inspired by the gods, traveled over something called land for years to reach the tower, overcoming great obstacles, such as giant convulsions of earth that required not only ascending but descending, too, and bodies of water so deep and wide that, to be crossed, vessels made of wood were required, with great wings like a bird that were sewn, of all things, from the fabric that we use to make shirts.

Since our people are descended from these heroic ancestors, we may be capable like them of great journeys. We may be able to climb not just eight floors but hundreds. In a single prolonged ascent, we might even climb all the way to the golden plain. Such a journey would require years of preparation and planning—our production of vegetables and meats, for example, would have to be increased, and our edibles would need to be preserved for the journey. And we would have to conserve our water more carefully, storing it for future use. But these are challenges that we might be able to overcome. If the sovereign called us to action, if the sovereign boldly proclaimed that we would together embark on an ambitious journey that would culminate in our collective apotheosis, we would stop grumbling and come together in this single purpose. The ambition and grandiosity of such an undertaking might be enough to excite even the most tired and cynical among us.

And so the tower inhabitants have mixed feelings toward the sovereign. Some believe that he may have good reasons for limiting the frequency and ambition of our ascents. For example, he may not believe that we are as strong as our ancestors. He may know us better than we know ourselves. He may think that our courage and fortitude have been damaged by hundreds of years in the tower. What happens to a man when his life is confined to a crowded chamber? When his diet consists of no more than a few vegetables, the scrawny flesh of chickens? When rude haulers barge in and out of his quarters hauling sacks of ashes and dirt? We have become a disagreeable people, suspicious of our neighbor and envious of his every crumb. We have lost our generosity and awe. The sunrises and sunsets move us no longer. Even the shifting imbrication of mists and cloudscapes, which, when we were children, fascinated us for hours, no longer compels us to wonder. This understanding of our character troubles the sovereign. More than anyone, he wants to bring about the deliverance of the people and the end to our long desiring. But as much as he yearns for the golden plain, he knows that our ascent must be gradual and deliberate. He has our interests at heart. He doesn't know how long the ascent will take and he understands that he cannot ask a civilization of men, women, and children, pigs and chickens, to abandon their chambers and terrace gardens and take to the stairs on what could be an exhausting and dangerous climb, and which could, after all, only worsen, not mend, the tensions within us.

Or perhaps, others believe, the sovereign limits our ascents because he suspects not his people but himself. He understands that such a journey would require a leader of great bravado and skill, and he questions his ability as a bellwether of the souls of men. He may be right. He has proven to be a competent sovereign, but his duties differ from that of a pioneer of towering heights. The sovereign is an administrator—and, as everyone readily admits, an excellent one. It is not easy to organize the lives of hundreds of thousands of people within a vast honeycomb of cells. The sovereign must track the number of births, the number of deaths, and the number of family members in each chamber and make adjustments to limit crowding and ensure cohesion. He must collect taxes and levy fines. He must regulate the upflow of soil from below onto the terraces and the outflow of produce from the terraces to the inner chambers. These are difficult tasks but not the same as the requirements of a great leader, rallying his people to press on against fatigue and confusion and against gravity itself and stagger in close quarters up an endless succession of stairs.

Then again—and it is surprising that no one has thought of this—maybe the sovereign fails to lead because he has suffered too long the disappointment of his ambitions. For each ascent, it is the sovereign who is naturally the first to climb new tower floors, the stairs carpeted in silk rugs dyed violet with the blood of roosters, while the sovereign's attendants bear upward with solemn ceremony the collection of treasures in trunks made of glass—the amethysts, the vessels of bergamot oil, the astrolabes, the taxidermied birds of yore with their great wings spread for flight—as the sovereign's women with their full hips and long, braided hair dance up the stairs chanting a song about the sun.

Certainly the sovereign cannot help but become excited by these festivities, growing hopeful of what he might find in his ascent, some new discovery that would suggest progress toward the pinnacle. But he is inevitably disappointed: the new chambers are identical to the old, made of the same smooth stone, cold and powdery to the touch—and the sovereign wanders through the open doorways from room to room, the empty caverns in their endless geometric configurations, and he is overwhelmed by melancholy and dread. He wonders, what is the purpose? Why with such fanfare and anticipation do we saddle ourselves to the stairs only to end in the same position as we began? Is it not better to cast off the promise of the golden plain and be satisfied with what we have? What if there is no pinnacle and no golden plain? Only this infinite column of emptiness and stone. What if there is no object for our ambitions? Perhaps, with each ascent, the sovereign is seeking not to bring his people closer to the golden plain but to provide the growing population with more space to live. The reason for the ascent is not eschatological but managerial.

And yet, though the sovereign may indulge in melancholy in those first moments after an ascent has been completed, when he must reconcile himself to his new surroundings so similar to the old, he is the sovereign after all, and is supposed to understand the gods' purposes. He remembers the legends of our people crossing land to arrive at the tower, exhorted by the gods. And he can hear these divine exhortations: standing at the corners of the tower, when certain conditions prevail, he can hear a hissing, almost liquid tremor, cold and shrill, in which some perceive a simple rhythm; others go so far as to call it a rhyme. At other times, the sound at the corners is different, a howling fusillade that inspires listeners to zeal. He may have had his fill of cloudscapes and sunsets but when the winds are blowing and the gods are singing at the corners of our tower, he is capable of reverence and celebration and he understands what it must be like to see beyond oblivion. At such moments, as tower inhabitants indulge in visions of the golden plain above, he finds himself imagining what might lie below: pastures where the stock might graze, unbroken bodies of water. He imagines the ground and its deep soil and the plants that are said to flourish from its surface, growing taller than anything that we might grow on our terraces, climbing into the air without effort or purpose.

Is this an absurd thing for a sovereign to do? To aspire not for the heavens but the earth? To contradict the claims of generations of scholars and argue that we've been pushing in the wrong direction? What if we should have been descending rather than ascending? What if the earth holds for us more pleasure than the golden plain? Maybe the problem is not ambition, as has been suspected, but the goal of our ambitions.

Perhaps it is impossible to know. The sovereign has only been the sovereign for a few decades. He must avoid rushing to any conclusions. He must examine the problem from all angles, never allowing his own personal failings to interfere with a scholarly analysis. He must eradicate himself from himself. After all, the wrong decision could be disastrous. If he exhorted his people to reverse course, we might descend the stairs for the rest of our lives and never come any closer to the ground than to the heavens. And he would hardly be able to bear the disgust as he moved among these lower peoples, some of whom do not know enough to throw their dung from the southern verges of the tower but throw it from the north, or do not throw out their dung at all but make of it some kind of powder and spread it over the soil. But this is impossible and I refuse to believe it; our life is not that ridiculous after all.

THE STUBBORN

Eliza Broadus, née Garland, who lived in a town called Iamonia in the wiregrass region of one of the southern states, married at twenty, pregnant at twenty-one, and still carrying the child into her twenty-third year. Eliza and her husband, Ephraim Broadus, lived with his parents in a notable home in a quiet district, not a decade after the War, close to downtown, where the horns of automobiles competed with the clip-clop of horses, wealthy vacationers mingled with farmers and shopkeepers, and the brick streets and brick buildings radiated the heat like a kiln. According to common reckoning, Eliza was more than six weeks past the time by which any reasonable woman would have given birth, and her belly showed. On the few occasions she left home, passersby would exclaim, with more reproach than enthusiasm: *Well I declare, Eliza, you* do *look overdue!*

These admonishments hardly concerned her, for she and her child, William, had reached an understanding. William was doing just fine where he was. His rhythms proceeded with hers, he slept with her through the night; when she woke, he woke, too. Awake, he was an active child—he didn't let the womb constrain him, and he was always up to something—slow, amniotic somersaults, umbilical tugs, kicking.

For entertainment, she invented games. She would tap on her belly and he would tap back. He learned to repeat the same number, up to four or five. He was the first unborn baby who could count. Other pastimes included the laughing game, the silly game, the dancing game. She hoped that her husband, Ephraim, might come to participate in these games, that someday he would be proud of William's accomplishments. But Ephraim was ashamed of her baby. Lately he had refused even to touch her belly. He was a good, honorable man and one day, she believed, he would have a change of heart. He would place his cheek on her belly and speak to William of his hopes and fears. Then the foolishness of the dream would occur to her, which made her laugh, this made William laugh, they enjoyed another round of the laughing game, he would laugh the longest and so prove victorious.

In this way Eliza passed the time beyond her nine-month, and it all might have gone on in pleasant continuity had it not been for her mother-in-law, Mrs. Broadus. Mrs. Broadus was a vigorous woman with curled, disorderly hair, which she tried to contain by snood or pompadour. She believed that babies should be born when babies are ordinarily born and she never ceased trying to arrange appointments for Eliza with midwife, herbalist, physician, faith healer. Eliza would reply that she appreciated Mrs. Broadus's concern but preferred to allow the baby to choose his own time of coming. "I don't understand why they call it expecting," she said to Mrs. Broadus. "As far as I know I'm not expecting anything at all."

Each morning at dawn Mrs. Broadus would arrive

unannounced in Eliza's room carrying the frond of a win-
tergreen fern, which she waved to freshen the air. She would
ask for a description of Eliza's condition and Eliza would
oblige: yes, she still felt burning "down there," and Mrs.
Broadus would remind her to try the lemon. "First thing
when you rise from bed," Mrs. Broadus would say, "before
you make water," and Eliza nodded, not admitting that she'd
taken a frantic liking to the taste of lemon, that her appetite
was changing—she'd lost the taste for game, preferred more
whimsical things: kumquats, slivered almonds. And yes, she
still had dizzy spells, no, not at the moment, yes, her ankles
remained swollen, and her eyes felt swollen and burned, but
no, this did not affect her vision, and yes, she still felt the
baby kicking.

Mrs. Broadus sensed that her daughter-in-law was being
less than forthcoming. She suggested to her son that he seek
help for his wife and child but Ephraim refused. He disagreed
with nearly all his mother's suggestions though he remained
deferential to his father. A nervous young man, Ephraim
Broadus, given to admiration of a few select men, a group
that included his father, and his boss, Murray Callahan, and
several officers of the Masonic Lodge. For nearly everyone
else—including himself—he felt a brittle disdain. His father
was a foreman for Callahan Mill and Lumber, a timber scout,
ranging over thousands of acres of wiregrass, braving rattlers
and wild boar, looking for straight grain among the longleaf
pine. Ephraim longed to work in the field with his father
but his health would not permit it—his respiration suffered

from exposure to the elements and so he manned a desk for Callahan filing invoices. Mr. Broadus prided himself on his good health and thought all physicians frauds. "The biggest threats to one's health are death and doctors," he liked to say, one of his many axioms, "but death at least is good enough to leave you alone until the proper time."

But if Ephraim Broadus, following his father, refused to intervene for the benefit of his child, Mrs. Broadus would not be deterred: at the next meeting of the Benevolent Society, she proposed that pregnancies lasting longer than ten months be banned.

"*Banned?*" asked Minerva Dorsey, president. Some of the less benevolent members of the Society snickered.

"Yes, banned," said Mrs. Broadus.

"My dear," said Minerva, "what should we do with these women, whose pregnancies continue longer than we prefer?" Mrs. Broadus replied that such women should be required to seek the opinion of a doctor or otherwise. "What do you mean by *otherwise?*" asked Minerva. Mrs. Broadus didn't know what she meant, but didn't have to, for, as she'd hoped, Lucille Callahan, wife of Murray Callahan, argued her side: While a ban might be too much, something must be done, for news of the peculiar case of Eliza Broadus was spreading and raising alarm among churches and societies throughout the region. It was an embarrassment to the respectable community of Iamonia. People were hinting that it was the work of the devil and his minions—that it was no child but some demon that was taking shape in the belly of Eliza Broadus.

A debate ensued. This was new territory for the Benevolent Society, which typically dealt with clear-cut moral issues like liquor and loose women and gambling. In the end a resolution was passed, rather than a ban, urging women with irregular pregnancies, including those longer than ten months, to seek professional help.

Afterward Mrs. Broadus worried to Mrs. Callahan that such a resolution, while not insignificant, would have little impact on her family.

"Don't you worry," said Mrs. Callahan. "I'm going to see to it that my husband helps Mr. Broadus adopt a more enlightened view."

The next day, a Thursday, Murray Callahan invited Mr. Broadus to lunch at the Chanticleer. Callahan never criticized his laborers, leaving that to his foremen, and he never criticized his foremen but over iced tea and oysters at the Chanticleer. "Look here now," he said to Mr. Broadus, "the human body is an organism. Hasn't anyone ever told you that? And like the longleaf pine, the body fails from time to time."

Mr. Broadus was not cowed by admonishment from Mr. Callahan as were other foremen; he did not grovel, tremble, or apologize. But he considered the only thing more valuable than health to be good sense, and he perceived that his views on the former were threatening his reputation for the latter. He acknowledged his mistake to his boss, and, that night, to his son as well.

"The mistake God deplores is the mistake we ignore," he

told Ephraim. Mr. Broadus sensed that he was not a natural leader of men, though he wished to be, and so as he labored in the forests he thought up these aphorisms, then employed them at the appropriate occasion, because he believed that by sounding wise he might lead where otherwise he might be inclined to follow. He spoke to Ephraim with his head lowered and his eyes fixed on something to the right, his jaw thrust open, slightly askew, which gave him a cagey look of mistrust, as if he suspected his family of complicity in some scheme.

Ephraim was incapable of criticizing his father; he did not view his father's new opinion on Eliza's delayed birth as a reversal so much as a refinement of his previous position. Later that night he informed Eliza of the news: Murray Callahan had kindly solicited the attention of a certain Dr. Harrocks, whose services were reserved for wealthy vacationers from the north but who'd offered to see Eliza at Callahan's behest. "It's generous of Mr. Callahan," said Ephraim, "you have to admit."

She admitted it.

"What's more," said Ephraim, "Mr. Callahan will pay the doctor's fee."

"That is very kind," admitted Eliza, and Ephraim agreed, impressed with the influence of his father, able to command the attention of a physician like Dr. Harrocks, who was famous as an exponent of the benefits of the wiregrass's aromatic pine breezes on lung disorders.

"But I don't have a lung disorder," said Eliza.

"How do we know for sure?" cried Ephraim. His voice trembled with exertion when he spoke—he always seemed to make great efforts to control himself in her company. At the dinner table he would hold her plate with both hands as he set it carefully before her.

"May I ask what is Dr. Harrocks's given name?" said Eliza.

"L. H."

"But, I am sorry, that is not a name."

"Important people don't have names," said Ephraim. "They have initials," and he tapped the tips of his fingers against each other with such force it made a sound like a tom-tom. His manic civility, nearly spasmodic in its intensity and forbearance, gave her a fright, and so she agreed to see the doctor.

The next day, Friday, as her mother-in-law cleaned for the doctor's arrival, Eliza was reading the *Times*. She took pleasure in reading it before anyone else, careful to fold it neatly, exactly as it had been, and return it to the foyer before Mr. Broadus came home from work. She skipped the editorials and the news and went straight to the booster contests. She'd always done well with these little challenges but recently she'd begun to find them more difficult: when she tried counting the number of *if*s on the front page, she couldn't concentrate and kept losing track. And the celebrity jingles of late had baffled her, until on this day she read: *I don't believe in time; I've put away my fears. What takes you nine months, may take me nine years. Or I'll keep expecting forever, which more of you should try: if our children are never born, neither can they die.* She read the jingle again, then read it out loud to William. What beasts, she thought. To make a jingle of my life like some hole-in-one golfer or scandalized councilman. That mocking supposition that William might never die, it made a travesty of just how precarious his life really was. "See?" she said to William. "You're right to want nothing to do with this world." When she heard Mrs. Broadus open the front door, heard her anxious, animated greeting and Dr. Harrocks's hearty reply, she limped out the kitchen door, crossed the yard, and climbed the stairs behind the garage to the long-vacant servant quarters above. The door was locked. She could hear Mrs. Broadus calling, but she ignored it. Hidden behind the garage, she lowered herself onto the stairs and spoke softly to William and was gratified to sense from him a subtle but decisive reply. He was fine—of course he was fine—why shouldn't he be? Her womb was able to provide for him everything that he required. Sitting on the top step of the small concrete landing, the shiny magnolia leaves crackling underneath her, she described to William everything he couldn't see: the lovely branches of flowering magnolia, the honeybees too fat to fly, the drifting colt-tail clouds, the glorious spring day. Through the trees she could see in the distance the Longley mansion, its brindle-brick façade and three-story Doric columns, a home Ephraim envied. She was intimidated by its size and austerity and imagined getting lost in its many rooms, separated from her child, wandering the halls, searching for him. She held her child in her belly, glad to have him close by (as she heard Ephraim walking down the circle drive and calling for her).

Nothing could be more natural than a mother's bond with her child. She knew for certain that William would never be born, that he was not held captive by some biological process gone awry but was the author of his own captivity (Ephraim walking through the garage below and calling), that William was not interested in being born, a decision he was free to make and she was powerless as well as reluctant to change.

Hours later, Eliza was driven by mosquitoes and fatigue back inside, returning as she left, through the kitchen. Mrs. Broadus stood at the stove, snapping the ends off green beans. "I knew you'd come back," she said. "Like I said to Mr. Broadus, where else is she going to go?" For several weeks, since her pregnancy had become public fodder at the mill, Mr. Broadus had preferred not to address Eliza directly, and so when he heard Eliza's return, he shouted out for Ephraim. Eliza could hear him from the sanctity of her bedroom down the hall, yelling at his wife and son. Was it their intent to get him fired? Murray Callahan would not appreciate his favors being ill-used. Dr. Harrocks had been put out of sorts and Mr. Broadus was humiliated. She could hear that Ephraim was replying but couldn't discern his words, then she heard Mrs. Broadus with her recalcitrant whine, then Mr. Broadus shouted, "I will not be party to the willful neglect of a child!"

The next day, Mr. Broadus went to work and Mrs. Broadus left to collect signatures for the Benevolent Society's electricity initiative. Rather than accompany his father to work, Ephraim left on what he would only describe to Eliza as an errand of great urgency. Eliza tried to do chores, sweeping, dusting, taking breaks to lie on her back or kneel on her hands and knees, a position that brought relief and that William enjoyed—she felt him hanging beneath her, swinging like a monkey from her spine. She hadn't waxed the kitchen floor in weeks, due to the effort involved, but today she did so, not because she felt especially strong but because she felt an obligation to this family: they had taken her in but been repaid with trouble. They had a right to expect a child, but since she couldn't fulfill their wishes, instead she waxed the floors.

When Ephraim returned, he took no notice of the floors but pulled from a brown bag two patent medicines: Parnell's Great Discovery (*Cures all diseases*) and DeWitt's Vegetable Compound for Women (*For every woman suffering from any ailment peculiar to her sex*). Eliza didn't like the bottles, their fervent claims, which suggested if not chicanery then delirium, a quality she saw in Ephraim's eyes. He mixed the DeWitt's with the Parnell's per the patent peddler's instructions. The peddler was well informed on women's troubles, Ephraim said. The peddler claimed that pregnancies occasionally lasted this long but the problem could be corrected with the right combination of elixirs. The peddler quoted a Bible verse as proof, which Ephraim didn't remember but that made reference to goats. "It's a matter of placental insufficiency," said Ephraim, quoting the peddler, "and that's something Parnell's and DeWitt's can solve. You can expect labor within twenty-four hours."

Eliza was discomfited by this strange green mixture, which fizzed unnaturally and smelled of alcohol. "All you have to do is drink," said Ephraim, tom-tomming his fingertips.

He looked unkempt, which was to say, disturbed: he had ventured into public with his sleeves rolled, and what's more, he was unshaved.

"I appreciate your thoughtfulness," said Eliza, "but my stomach is unwell."

Ephraim held up the Parnell's. "Cures all," he said. "Even stomachaches."

"I better not."

"This is the thing with placental insufficiencies," said Ephraim. "Something has to be done or the placenta becomes more and more insufficient."

"I appreciate your thoughtfulness," said Eliza and she was struck by the coarse handsomeness of his unshaven face, which made him seem more decisive than usual. Wasn't he making great efforts on her behalf? And wasn't the purpose of childbearing to send the child out into the world? She was being selfish. Let the world do what the world wants to do—the Benevolent Society and its decrees. Why fight it? My child is mine and I am his. This comforted her. A parent can't make a child do what he doesn't want to do, and William was a stubborn child. If he wanted, he would stay in her womb no matter what fantastical potions she imbibed. He'd already shown himself stronger than nature—what threat this harmless mixture everyone but Ephraim knew was just alcohol and tonic, a lump of sugar, nothing William couldn't handle. In two gulps she swallowed it down.

———

In half an hour she was passed out at the table. Ephraim carried her to bed. She slept through the night and past noon. When she woke, she didn't recognize her surroundings. A bedroom, but not hers, and very dark: through the window, the sunlight refracted through the leaves of an overlarge, ominous shrub. All was well with William—he slept—though all wasn't well otherwise, her eyes burned, head throbbed, mouth waterless and stale as if coated with some inhuman residue. The mattress was too soft; she was enveloped in cushioning. Her back ached. She groaned then heard an unexpected rustle, a hand at her back. It was Ephraim. He pulled her up and fluffed her pillows. She sat up and saw it all more clearly now—his room, not hers. Mrs. Broadus had insisted on furnishing the couple with their own spacious bedroom, decorating it with all the usual feminine gewgaws—roseate mirrors and frosted lampshades with grapes cut into the glass, a garden of floral pillows. Ephraim couldn't stand the decor, and so he remained in his own room, the room he'd grown up in, purged of all ornament or keepsake, a small study with a coal fireplace dark with soot, the desk bare and chairless.

"Well?" he said. "Labor pains?"

None. On the contrary, while all about her felt unsteady, uncertain, William lay secure and enfolded and burning warm inside her, like a hot tin held between cupped hands.

"What happened?" she asked.

"I stayed up all night with you. Pacing. Are you sure—nothing at all?"

She shook her head. The vigil had done him little good. He remained unshaven, which Eliza no longer found appealing, the hair grown in unevenly, face cast in shadows.

"Mother says it must be some demon that you've got there, trapped in the womb," he said. "My God, it's impossible! Dr. Harrocks is baffled."

"Dr. Harrocks?" said Eliza.

"Baffled."

"You permitted him to examine me?"

"While you were sleeping. I assumed you wouldn't mind."

"I see."

"It was all done courteously, with respect to your privacy."

She saw that he had tricked her. He said that it wasn't deliberate. On his way home from the peddler's, he had sought the doctor, who made no promises but said he might drop by, and as it happened, he dropped by later that afternoon, while Eliza was asleep. Yes, he could've woken her, and yes, he could've turned the doctor away, but he assumed Eliza was merely shy, he'd meant well, and besides, what harm had come of it? What did she expect them to do, pace all night for months, gnaw their fingernails until they bled, waiting for nothing, while their baby languished and all Iamonia wondered? A baby coming this late, according to the doctor, would grow slowly, he would be sickly, of unexceptional character. But he was alive, if not hearty, and might be saved if they intervened right away.

"Excuse me, may I ask what is it you mean—intervene?" said Eliza.

Ephraim hesitated. "These aren't ancient times," he said. "Dr. Harrocks is very advanced in his field."

"Is that your opinion?" asked Eliza.

"Tell me the truth, Eliza. Not some dreamy fantasy! Am I to really believe you? Do you really know what you're doing?"

Eliza hesitated. Lately William had begun acting strangely, sleeping through the night and morning without stirring. Afternoons she could feel him rousing, but his activity was short-lived and lacked vigor. She feared she'd made some terrible mistake. Was she wrong to trust herself over the opinions of strangers? Had she misunderstood William's desires? This possibility beyond all others dismayed her. Then she felt a familiar nudge from within and her faith was confirmed. "Yes," she said, and she invited Ephraim to feel her belly for himself but he refused.

"Look me in the eyes, Eliza!"

She looked him in the eyes.

"Jesus Christ, tell me the truth!"

She told him the truth.

"Jesus Christ!" he said as if in anger, but if it was anger it was not directed at her.

Soon after in the living room, Eliza heard Ephraim confronting his parents—something she'd never heard him do before. If that carriage arrived from the hospital tomorrow morning, he would not let them take Eliza away. Surgery carried too many risks. Mr. Broadus, surprised by the challenge, responded with an axiom: *A drowning man is not troubled by rain.*

"My wife's life or death isn't the same thing as a little rain!" shouted Ephraim, with such maniacal humility it might have been a shriek. And then, managing to regain some modicum of control, "I'm sorry, but did you ever consider, Father," he said, and Eliza could hear his voice trembling, hear him struggling, "that there's not an adage for everything?"

Mr. Broadus said, "Your wife requires the assistance of a professional."

"She's not a cadaver, to cut open as you please!"

"He's a surgeon, Ephraim," said Mrs. Broadus, "not a murderer. God sent him to help us."

"God's done enough already!" said Ephraim.

"Don't be scandalous!" said Mr. Broadus. "The entire town is in agreement."

"But I am not in agreement."

"You're an employee of Callahan Mill and Lumber," said Mr. Broadus.

"It's not the business of Callahan, it's my business, mine to decide!"

"Oh? And what have you decided?" asked Mr. Broadus.

"I don't know yet," said Ephraim. He couldn't escape the notion, which he'd never encountered in quite this way before, that his father's best qualities, his courage, his command, his wisdom, might not be the qualities required to resolve this particular problem. His hands went cold and his jaw throbbed: If his father couldn't solve the problem, what chance did he have to do so, a desk clerk with nervous hands afflicted with debilitating allergies? His wife required from him strength and constancy and he had neither. Eliza entered the room, unsteady on stiff, swollen legs. He gestured to her spasmodically and said to his parents, "See? See?" It was unclear what he meant to be seen but that his wife was suffering under a terrible burden.

Mrs. Broadus pointed at Eliza and said, "I've got a bottle of laudanum and a forged blade and if that doctor doesn't do it I will free that child myself!"

"Lottie Broadus!" said Mr. Broadus.

"No one touches her but me," said Ephraim and he led her away by the arm.

They spent the remaining hours before bed together in her room. He was an unfamiliar presence here—uncomfortable. He yanked one of her chairs off the floor, carried it over to the door as if he meant to sit there, guarding her room from trespassers, yet as soon as he sat he was up again, unable to keep still. He kept lifting the keepsakes off her desk and setting them down again without having looked at them. He said that none of this was her fault—obviously, he knew that—and yet each time he said it, he seemed to believe it less. It was *someone's* fault—that much was certain—only he didn't know whose. He smelled dinner cooking and offered to bring her some, which she kindly refused. He reproached himself—of course this was no time to eat. Then a quarter hour later he left abruptly and returned with a plate of fried chicken, which he never touched, and a glass of water, which he offered to Eliza but gulped himself until it was gone.

THE STUBBORN

He insisted that he would sleep on the floor but that night she woke to find him lying beside her. There was abundant room for two in the marriage bed that Mrs. Broadus had bought for them, but he crowded against her; her bare knees touched the cold surface of the wall. She wore only her shift. She had never felt his hand so nakedly on her breast. Her back was to him and though he held her gently, the discomfort was intense, her engorged breasts sensitive to the lightest touch. She moved his hand away. He moved it to her hips, pulling closer. He did not appear to be dressed. William was stirring, he yawned and stretched, curled to face her, clutching her spine like a charm. Ephraim lifted her shift and held her bare hips, pulling closer. In another time, Eliza had yearned for this, the pleasure one body shared with another. But now it was all wrong. She removed his hand from her hip and placed it on her belly. He moved it back.

"We have to," he hissed. "It's what you do to induce."

"No," she said. William was growing agitated, he kicked fitfully; her kidneys took the blows. He clutched the walls of her uterus with such ferocity she cried out in pain.

"It won't take long," Ephraim hissed.

"No," said Eliza.

"You want the doctor's intrusion tomorrow, or mine tonight?" But he was already intruding and Eliza couldn't resist. She bit her fist as her bare knees hit the wall.

Afterward he left her alone in bed, he lay on the floor. He woke and heard her quiet, heaving breaths. "Eliza, is it all right?"

he asked but she didn't reply. Amid the haunt of muffled sounds and the crude dance of shadows on the walls, he lay, listening to her breaths. It seemed to him that pregnancy was a terrible human ritual with no rationale—why did people put themselves through such misery? The entirety of life was waiting for things that you didn't need and could never have. Again he called her name but now he heard no breaths at all until she gasped and the bed shook and he leapt up and clutched at her shoulders. "Let me get the light," he said but she grabbed his wrist. "The light, Eliza!" but she wouldn't let go of his wrist. Only hours ago he had taken her by force but now he could not break his wrist from her grip. Dizzy, he fell forward and his free hand caught himself on the bed. He felt the warm wetness of the sheet and knew it was blood. He broke his hand loose and lit the lamp. She was lying curled on the mattress in a wallow of blood. Her belly was taut and glossy as blown glass, the sheet was twisted at her feet. She was lying only a few feet away but seemed to be marooned among some great expanse. He saw the thoughtlessness of what he'd done, trying to induce the birth of a child grown so large it could not slip free from the womb.

She clutched her arms to her chest and spoke softly to William, unable to hear from him any reply. Ephraim stood beside her. He told her to stay calm but she couldn't. He told her to take big breaths but she couldn't. "Do me a favor?" she said. He nodded. "Will you place your hand on my belly and tell me what you feel?"

He didn't look at her but unbuttoned his cuffs, rolling

up each sleeve, as if she hadn't asked him to touch her belly but plunge his hands deep into something unknown. She closed her eyes and felt the cold tips of his fingers like the blunt ends of some metal medical instrument. He would not look at her but kept his fingertips resting lightly on the tight surface of her belly. She suggested he lay his hands flat so he could feel with his palms and he did. She thought she felt William respond languidly to the new sensation, like some creature roused by light to rise from the depths of the sea to the surface.

"What do you feel?" she asked.

"I don't know—what am I supposed to feel?"

"A gesture," she said. "A flutter." Hadn't she felt William moving? Hadn't he frolicked inside her, rolling about like some wild circus tumbler? Or had she imagined everything, the exuberant life of her child, who now seemed no more than some lifeless bulge growing like a cyst inside her. Who knew what was happening inside her body? She felt dry, depleted, as if hollowed out by a hot wind. Her belly cramped in one massive heave and cramped again.

Ephraim was speaking. It seemed he had been speaking for some time. The feeble overgrowth of beard, the blunt, imperfect brink of his forehead, eyes wide, he looked at her. There was something strange in his visage, something affirmative that she'd never seen before. He seemed to have been inspired by some spasm of imagination, like a vision he'd remembered from distant times. His hand remained on her belly and it was moving across her belly and he was describing what he felt. Yes, he said, he could indeed—he could feel their child in his hands: here is his head, it feels oddly solid and oblong, like a turnip. And here is his bony neck like the taproot descending. What wild red hair, he said, how he has grown. He's not compliant like he was before. He's learned to insist on his turn. "I've got his hand in mine," said Ephraim, "he's got a firm grip but he knows when to let it go. Can you feel that, Eliza? Can you feel him letting go?"

Eliza smiled. "Everything good is like a snare," she said. "The good never lets you go."

THE WATCH

The watch was a gift from her father, two months before he died. Ordinarily he was not a taciturn man but about the watch he had little to say. One day he simply gave it to her, with no explanation, nor was there any occasion for the gift. He left it on the kitchen table with a note—*For Marie*—and when asked about it afterward would only say that he had found the watch by way of somewhat extraordinary circumstances and that she should have it. She was touched by the gift—so rare for her father, the sentimental gesture—but though she tried, she couldn't bring herself to appreciate it. She preferred modern jewelry, insomuch as she wore jewelry at all, but this was an antique. The silver band shimmered; the small pearl face was circumscribed by a silver ring and the hours were designated by beads that gleamed like mercury. It was too showy for her taste. That her father had wanted her to have this particular watch surprised her—he had no affinity for glitter nor did he indulge, as had her mother, in nostalgia for the glories of the Gilded Age. All the same, she might have brought herself, had it been a bracelet or necklace in a similar style, to wear it on occasion, but she did not like to wear a watch and had not since she was a child. To check a watch frequently—as her colleagues did—was meant to communicate a sense of your own importance (I really am quite busy and have only a minute longer . . .) but in fact revealed an anxiety about the passing of time.

That is why, she told herself, she did not wear her father's watch.

Shortly after her father gave her the watch he announced his illness and shortly after that he died. The illness was so vicious and efficient, there was no question of lifesaving measures. Only a palliative diet of mortal painkillers and he was gone. She was an orphan. She felt lonely, betrayed, humiliated, like the girl jilted by her date at the dance. Then her grief was upstaged by her guilt and she fixated on the watch: Would it have been so much trouble for her to wear it in his company?

A few weeks after her father's death, on the first morning that Marie decided to wear the watch, her daughter noticed. "It doesn't work," she observed.

"Nonsense," said Marie. But it was true. The second hand was still.

"Try winding it," said her husband and she wound it.

"That did the trick," said Marie.

"I don't like it," said her daughter. This did not come as a surprise—her daughter didn't care for many of her mother's fashion choices. "It's too shiny—like a spoon. Are you really going to wear it?"

Only eight, her daughter had already developed a number of fashion rules. She refused to wear orange because it brought out something like scurvy in her complexion. She refused to wear leggings under her dresses in winter: she preferred to be pretty even if cold. She referred to her T-shirts as *blouses*. She insisted on choosing her own clothes each evening and laid them out in the chair. Other mothers said this was charming; Marie told herself that all children have their idiosyncrasies. But when her daughter criticized her own clothing she felt inadequate. Marie did not attend to her wardrobe with as much diligence as other professional women, but she thought she had a certain style: pencil skirts, leather boots, blouses with attractive necklines. But her daughter thought these outfits boring and wanted from her mother not a style that was extravagant or tawdry as you might expect of a girl that age but something effortless, something exalted. The girl wanted to be awed. She intuited in fashion the potential for transformation and Marie couldn't help but feel, subjected to her daughter's scrutiny, that she had failed some test not as a mother but as a human being.

Marie took off the watch and turned to her son, who, chin just clearing the table, was eating his breakfast with a dutifulness that Marie found touching. She let the watch dangle in front of him; he dropped his spoon in the oatmeal and looked to her with wonder. Playfully swatting at the watch, he flourished a grin. "Pretty!" he shouted, and though Marie knew it was absurd—the boy was three—she felt her fashion sense and her human competence vindicated.

The next morning her daughter pointed out again that the watch wasn't working. And she claimed that it was stuck on the same time as before—3:27.

"A.M. or P.M.?" asked her husband.

"What difference does it make?" snapped Marie. Having chosen to wear the watch, she was experiencing a change in perspective—she felt defensive about it as a mother might of a child and she didn't want to hear it subjected to analysis.

"It makes a big difference," he said, with that ironic look of mystery that he employed when he was being pedantic. But he did not elaborate, assuming that only he would be interested in the distinction. She preferred to let the matter drop but her daughter prodded him to go on. He explained that if the watch stopped at 3:27 in the afternoon, then it was at the end of a twelve-hour cycle and was probably getting stuck on some glitch. But if it had stopped at 3:27 in the morning, then that, it seemed to him (though he was no watchmaker), was harder to explain: getting stuck at the same point in every other cycle—every twenty-four hours instead of every twelve—made little mechanical sense. It was a fair point (damn him) but she did not have time to consider it: the kids were late for school.

Over the course of the morning and early afternoon, ensconced in her office at her husband's architectural firm, redrafting the second-story layout on the Polhill project, she thought of the watch. Had it been broken when her father gave it to her? Or had it developed the flaw afterward? It hadn't occurred to her, when she received the watch, to check that it was functional. That was rational. Time wasn't one of her enthusiasms. Neither were maps and directions. Had her father given her a GPS, like the watch, she would have thrown it in a drawer. The question of whether her father knew of the flaw seemed to her of overriding importance, for it had some bearing on his intentions. Being honest, she had to admit that perhaps she had not worn the watch for him when he was dying because she suspected that he was trying to convey a message with the gift beyond sentiment and she did not like what she thought he was trying to say. Though her father was quick to express his political opinions, personal confrontation agitated him and he avoided criticizing his loved ones except through indirection. When her mother intended to wallpaper the master suite, her father brought home a new easy chair for the room in strongly contrasting colors, claiming an aching back. A day after Marie informed her parents that she was planning to travel to Cambodia—this was right after the coup—her father totaled his car, bruising four ribs and dislocating a hip. He'd never had an accident—a cautious driver—and could not explain why he was driving fifty-five three blocks from home in a quiet neighborhood. It seemed vain to suppose that he would put himself through such an ordeal on her account, yet his message, if there was a message, presented itself with perverse clarity: if she wanted to enjoy herself at great risk and expense, well, he could do that, too. She went to Cambodia anyway, and was made miserable not so much by the conditions but by her inability to find a working international phone to call home and, above all, by the guilt.

Supposing her father had been trying to tell her something with the watch, what was it? She had her suspicions.

Though he was otherwise a reliable liberal, one of his favorite topics was the laziness and unreliability of what he called the washed-out class. He complained that their lack of ambition was evident in their demeanor, behavior, clothes, accessories. Have you ever noticed, he would say, how kids these days never wear a watch? The watch was an essential component of the ambitious professional's wardrobe. Her father might have been reminding her with the watch that time was running out for her career as an architect and that she was not as ambitious—or not as successful—as she could have been. But if he had knowingly given her a watch that didn't work—well, that changed the message altogether.

Remembering her husband's distinction—A.M. or P.M.?—she waited with increasing anxiety to see if the watch would work beyond 3:27 in the afternoon. She attempted various tasks—drafting new plans or revising old ones, deciphering arcane building codes, emailing colleagues—but she kept checking the watch. Its appearance was growing on her—the tight weave of the silver band was more intricate than she'd first observed and the clasp had an ingenious and elegant design that hid the mechanism within. The pearl face was pleasantly ethereal and the hands of the watch, long and thin as filaments, turned with delicacy and precision. She could hear her husband laughing with one of the secretaries in the hall—something about slicing an apple with a butter knife—and at one point the electricity in the office fluttered and went out and there was a jovial collective groan when the lights came back on and the computers rebooted, and the afternoon yawned and the spectacle of time displayed itself in all its zeal and tedium and finally she watched as the moment drew near and the watch ticked calmly beyond the appointed minute and hour.

So it was not something so simple as a mechanical glitch. The watch could tick happily past 3:27 in the afternoon but past 3:27 at night it would not go. She registered the discovery with unease. She didn't like mysteries. But she told herself that it wouldn't do to get hysterical, it was only her grief at the loss of her father finding expression in a new way.

That night she and her husband settled in to read in bed—he had a book about the Spanish Civil War, and she was halfway through a gloomy novel about a doomed affair in Sierra Leone. Only in the last few months had she been able to establish a consistent bedtime routine for her children that allowed her the time and energy to turn to a book at the end of the day, and now she was pleased with herself for putting aside her anxieties and she read several chapters before she realized that she wasn't reading but thinking. The watch had gotten her thinking about her father. She was thinking about how strong and calm he was in general but how, when provoked in a certain way or concerned about a certain event that, often as not, seemed insignificant, he would grow irritable and his hands would shake and he would say the most illogical or insensitive things. She was thinking about how she would respond to him at such times—with indignation, because she couldn't change the standard by which she ordinarily judged him. She often grew affronted in a similar way with her children when they acted irrationally—that was something she must correct. She must learn to respond more maturely to the burden of her responsibilities. As she was thinking along these lines, it occurred to her that she could hear the watch ticking. This was peculiar—she'd never heard it tick before. There had been no apparent change in the ambient noise of the bedroom—it was too early in the season for the furnace to run and the washer and dryer, the dishwasher, too, were silent—but though the watch had been ticking all along, she only heard it now. And now that she heard the watch, it was impossible to ignore. Its message was too insistent. She felt a momentary panic listening to the ticking of the watch and she put it in the bedside drawer.

She woke in the middle of the night. She'd been dreaming about something obscure that posed a threat, it seemed, for her children. Without looking at the clock she guessed the time. In the dark she drew open the drawer and listened for the watch. She listened a long while, waiting for the silence to settle and the ticking to appear in her hearing like a figure rounding a bend and approaching in the wood. But there was no ticking. The watch had stopped. It was half past three.

In the dark, she treated her dry eyes with the drops then wound the watch and put it on. She was still trying to understand what the watch might signify—in the way it functioned perfectly one moment and was struck dumb the next, it seemed a willful reminder of the perversity of time, how suddenly life could go awry. That had happened to her father. But this was a grim message to impart to one's daughter with a gift, and not much like her father, who avoided existential questions. Nevertheless, she couldn't escape the notion that the watch was a reminder of the sudden misfortune that might come to her or her family and she checked on her sleeping children—first son, then daughter. She noticed in her daughter's room that the cords of the venetian blinds were hanging too low and she wrapped them around the valance. An unnecessary precaution for an eight-year-old but she knotted them for good measure. The girl slept warm to the touch and eschewed blankets. Unlike her brother, she slept angelically, with her hands folded peaceably on her chest, one leg straight and the other bent, both feet pointing elegantly as if executing a pirouette. But the pose didn't fool Marie—though well behaved, her daughter was going to be the problem child. She lacked the acquiescent temperament that Marie had as a girl and she was capable of covert acts of vengeance and prolonged sulking. Her eyes frequented the ground and seemed to nurse some metaphysical irritation. Her judgments of her mother could be sudden and severe. The girl was already cultivating the two qualities that a young woman needs to become a successful professional: ambition and indifference to the needs of others. Marie had never been able to muster much indifference, but as a graduate student, she'd been full of ambition. What happened? Had her concerns for her children supplanted her concern for work, or had her children exposed that she never had much interest in work in the first place?

She continued to pursue a professional career but without

her husband's support she would have had no career at all. Four years ago, he left Kedlick & Rouse to start his own firm, specializing in energy-efficient historic renovations. At the time he insisted on making her partner and she had agreed, though she knew she did not have a body of work deserving such an honor, and, pregnant with her second child, that she would not be able to complete such work in the near future. She hated feeling as if she had benefited from nepotism, hated feeling as if she had to justify herself to her colleagues, who treated her with perfectly amiable respect but who, she learned from her husband's secretary, were not above questioning her commitment to a particular project or attempting to take over from her certain responsibilities. It was true—she required more time than her colleagues to complete a draft. But that was because she was thorough. It had become the trend to draft toward the big idea, to impress with originality and flair, leaving the thankless work of reconciling the design with impediments to hapless subordinates. Her husband was guilty of this. Not Marie—she labored over every detail. Unlike her husband, she did not enjoy drafting. But she did enjoy the satisfaction of doing a good job, of having her good work recognized. She still had the ability to become absorbed in a project but she'd found this more difficult as her thoughts fixated on her children. There were appointments for the boy with the pediatrician, who held that he didn't have asthma but Marie suspected otherwise. And since her daughter had split up with her best friend, Marie had been meeting with her second-grade teacher regularly to ensure that she was making new friends. Not only were her children the cause of anxieties but guilty pleasures, too: more than once she had slipped out of the office to observe, at a distance, her boy playing a few blocks away at preschool. He was a wild one on the playground, hurling himself off the swings into the abyss. At such moments she shared his exhilaration and nearly collapsed out of fear for his safety. Once she'd positioned herself too close, and he spotted her and she'd had no choice but to say hello, tousle his wispy hair. When she'd left him at the fence with the teacher he'd broken into a fit of hysterics and she felt as though she had made some terribly irresponsible error that any sensible parent would have avoided. The teacher did little to dispel the notion.

That afternoon at lunch she walked to a jewelry shop downtown. "Scientifically," said the jeweler, "what you say is impossible. A man can go wrong lots of ways but a watch only goes wrong a few ways and a watch can't go wrong like that." Would he look at it anyway? Sure, he wasn't a man to say never but he wasn't a man to make promises either and he would charge for the time whether he fixed the watch or not.

"Can you look at it this afternoon? It was a gift from my father and I'd rather not leave it overnight."

"But overnight is when you have the problem—correct?" She nodded. "It's like the car that only makes the noise when it's gone from the shop. Consider I'm your mechanic. I've got to see the problem with the machinery after it fails."

She left the watch overnight. All the same she woke at

half past three as she had the night before and she worried over the watch as for a sick child. She had trouble going back to sleep and couldn't concentrate long enough to read. Her husband slept. He generally slept on his back with his mouth open but now he was on his stomach, face buried in pillows—he liked his pillows soft and it was hard to see how he managed to avoid suffocating but she could hear his easy breathing. Had the fire alarm sounded or a pane of glass crashed or some other threat to the household broken the silence he would have woken immediately, but the disturbances created by his wife and children did not disturb him. Not even when their daughter in her infancy had caterwauled with nightmares had her husband awoken. He was not indifferent to his children's suffering but comfortable with the differing parental roles that husband and wife had assumed. He fulfilled his fatherly responsibilities with dutifulness, not to say gusto, and he was content to leave his wife to the fulfillment of hers.

She checked on her daughter, then son. She couldn't bring herself to leave the boy's room and remained with him, curled in the rocker like a schoolgirl with her knees to her chest and her hands clasped round her shins. Such a good little sleeper—he rarely woke. But his arms and legs, as was often the case, were twisted into a contortionist's pose and his face bore the ashen expression of the grave. It frightened her to watch him sleep. She thought of the time that her father had taken her to the cabin and they had arrived after the two-hour drive to find that he had forgotten the key. The darkness billowed in like a fog from the high mountains, and her father, suddenly unnerved in his frantic way, circled the cabin three times prying at windows and kicking at doors until with no warning he took hold of a tire iron and smashed it through a window. Her window. He told her to wait while he climbed through and she heard the glass on her bed breaking underfoot. She was nine years old. He changed her sheets and vacuumed and mopped up every particle of glass, and he taped a towel over the window and read her three chapters from the book and even offered to let her sleep in his room but none of it assuaged her fear. So effortless, it had been for him, to shatter the glass, so effortless and aggressive, those long crystal daggers dangling from the sash and the dark figure of the man looming in her window. She was terrified that something so familiar could become in an instant something so frightening. Her father slept in the chair beside her all night and she found his presence comforting but also disturbing and she stayed awake though she pretended to sleep. Later her mother scolded him—why hadn't he asked the neighbors for the spare key? Her broken window could have been avoided if he had only stayed calm.

Now, remembering her fear, she watched her son frozen in his peaceful contortions and she was overwhelmed, as her father must have been, by a prophecy of her own failures.

While she was away from her desk, the jeweler left a voice message: she could pick up the watch anytime. She was irritated that he gave no indication of the outcome—no diagnosis, no cure—but she reminded herself that it was only a watch. She planned to pick it up at the end of the workday on her way to get the children, but her husband came in at four—they had an unfavorable injunction from the building commission on the Polhill project and they needed to revise her drafts right away. She told him that was impossible. She knew exactly why the building commission had objected and had warned of this very thing. It would take days to revise the project properly. He laughed—an effortless, prolonged laugh, which he employed when he was grateful or relieved but also, in this case, to put her at ease. Even in moments of high professional stress, he possessed a sorcerer's calm. Choosing his words carefully, he said that Polhill was quite upset and threatening to cancel the project unless they got him a solution right away. Perhaps she could pass the drafts on to Rawlins?

"Rawlins," she said.

"Or McCollum. Someone with a fresh eye." And then casually, as if as an afterthought, "We need the drafts by seven, that's all."

She understood that she was being patronized—he would prefer to give the work to Rawlins, a pimple-faced associate with the caffeine addict's erratic hand, or to McCollum, who left smudges like paw prints all over the page, rather than take a chance on her finishing the work under pressure. She took a sip of water, trying to stay calm. Her lips were dry and despite the water they instantly felt dry again. Her husband stepped inside her office and nudged at the door with his foot. I'm listening to you, he was trying to say by the gesture—but having failed to shut the door completely he revealed that his attention was elsewhere. He waited before her desk with equanimity, betraying nothing. She suspected that he didn't feel such a thing as apprehension at all but rather experienced the urgency of time passively, robustly, as the sea was moved by the gentle and unremitting influence of the moon.

She told him that she would try to finish a very rough draft by seven—but he would have to pick up the kids. And the watch. "Very well," he said without hesitation. He even managed to look pleased. "You can drop them off with Polhill on your way home."

She did not finish the drafts by seven. It was not a failure of concentration, not a failure of will nor of skill nor desire. She worked with quiet and painstaking haste. She reviewed the unfavorable injunction and executed a flawless revision of the draft that left no possibility unaccounted for, that for every question provided a sensible and original solution. The finest burst of work she'd managed in years. She felt pride in the work, which would prove to her husband and Polhill and the cadre of sycophants lurking in the halls that she was a gifted architect after all. But she also suffered from the perception that she had neglected her family for the sake of her vanity. It was a quarter past nine. With some direction, McCollum could have handled the job (if not Rawlins), and she could have spent the evening at home with her children. There was no telling whether her husband would have managed to get them properly to bed. It was preposterous, she knew, even superstitious, but she couldn't help agreeing with her children that their welfare depended in part on the scrupulous completion—in the correct order—of every part of their respective bedtime rituals.

Arriving home, she found that all was quiet—the children were evidently in bed. She wanted to kiss them good night but it was not good policy to look in on them at such an hour for fear of disturbing them before they'd fallen sound asleep. She prepared herself a drink and found her husband in bed with his book. "Polhill just called," he said. "He's very pleased. Aggravated with the situation, but pleased with the result."

She handed him an envelope with copies of the drafts. "Have a look," she said.

"Tomorrow."

"Don't you want to see them?"

"Oh, I'm sure they're excellent." And he laughed his effortless, prolonged laugh to indicate that he, like Polhill, was pleased—but unlike Polhill, his interest in the drafts could wait. Then he adjusted his glasses and returned to his book. Marie held the drink. She didn't care for liquor and wasn't sure why she'd prepared a drink except it seemed the thing to do. She was only now coming down from the ordeal and a clammy exhaustion was setting in. Her husband's lack of interest in her work seemed indicative not of a reliable pragmatism as she might have ordinarily understood it, but of a pessimism that indulged in no expectations of others, of a love that, in its facile refusal to understand her worth and fears, bordered on bigotry. She stared at him and said, "Is that all?"

He looked up from his book but didn't answer.

She said, "Is there anything else about the day that you'd like to discuss?"

"Sure," he said. "What did you have in mind?" In his lap, he kept the book open—holding out for the possibility that he might return to it.

"Didn't you pick up the watch?"

"Oh yes. There—on the dresser."

"Did he fix it?"

"Hmm." He laughed. "You know it didn't occur to me to ask."

This elicited from her an acid, rueful smile. "Of course not," she said. "Why should you?"

He thought a moment, started to reply but stopped. It was as if he had seen the various ways he might quibble with her remark and had, reluctantly, put each aside. "Come to bed," he said. "You've put yourself through quite a day."

His condescension irritated her. What did he know about her day? And what made him think that coming to bed would help? "I can't sleep!" she cried.

"Because of your father's broken watch?" He was making an effort, but he could not hide the fact that the watch was little more for him than a technical curiosity, like the radio that picks up a phone conversation a dozen floors below—the kind of thing that happens at random in a globe crisscrossed with electrodes and circuitry. She took a swallow from her drink—too much vermouth. She swished the liquid in the glass and took another swallow and another. The lips, the tongue, the cave of membranes at the back of her throat felt dry and shrunk as an old sponge.

"Don't you think it's possible," she said, "that my father gave me the watch on purpose? That he was trying to tell me something?"

"What do you mean?"

"I mean maybe he knew about the flaw. Maybe he was even responsible for it—he found a jeweler who could alter the watch in that way or he took a class on watchmaking and did it himself."

"But why?"

"To teach me a lesson."

"Christ, Marie." He shut the book, set it down. "Do you really think your father would do that? Maybe it's just a watch."

"But—think about it," she said, and she told him her theory—that the watch was a reminder of how suddenly life could go wrong. The formulation was too simple but she wanted to startle her husband—wanted to impress upon him the enormity of her apprehensions. She said that was her father, too—healthy one day, dying the next. But the mention of her father, though only intended as a rhetorical gambit, unexpectedly touched at the heart of the matter, and now she was crying and she was talking about her fears for herself and her loved ones, of her fear that someone of great importance to her would fail. All these years, she said, she'd been unable to commit herself to her career because she was saving herself for the day when she would be needed by her family. What would have been the point of all that ambition and effort to build a portfolio, she said, when all of it, at any time, all of it could just be nullified by a sudden accident or illness and she would have to devote herself to someone else?

She didn't go on. She was stopped by the look on her husband's face—that look of aggrieved amazement at what he perceived to be the foibles of the female sex, with the tight dark curls clinging to his forehead, his blue eyes holding her gaze and his hand settled on the closed book as if taking an oath. He was not deliberately unsympathetic, rather, his tendency was to offer practical solutions—drink chamomile, get more exercise—but he'd learned that such suggestions in such circumstances were best left unsaid.

"Look," he said, suddenly brightening with an idea. "Probably the jeweler did fix it. It's possible. He's a professional, after all."

She could tell that he meant it sincerely and that only disheartened her more.

At 3:27 that night, the watch stopped. She knew when it stopped because the watch was not in the drawer but on her wrist and because she was listening while her husband slept and she heard the last tick. Rather, she did not hear the last tick but she heard the sepulchral sound of the watch not ticking, that voluminous silence of the house at night that in the past she had found so peaceful but that now seemed to foretell some misfortune and that reminded her, in a home full of loved ones, that she was alone. She wound the watch, winding, winding, with a frantic maternal conviction that she must dedicate herself to its care. She lay still in bed. She fought the impulse to check on the children. It was not the night but the day that posed the greatest threat to their safety yet she left them all day to the care of strangers so that, with halfhearted enthusiasm, she could struggle at her career. The dark room was illuminated by the colorless glow of the streetlight from behind the blinds. With her eyes open she could manage but when she closed them she was afflicted with inchoate thoughts, the throes of dreams. She sat up, trying to stay calm. She treated her dry eyes with the drops. A remnant of the drink remained and she swallowed it down.

She checked on her daughter first, sleeping on her back with arms akimbo. She'd taken to wearing her hair in a long, thickly braided ponytail that her husband had forgotten to unbraid for the night. Marie checked to see whether he'd adjusted the vent, whether he'd turned the blinds. To her surprise, he'd remembered both. For all her frustration with him, he was a competent father. With her eyes accustomed to the dark she could see everything. It was extraordinary, it seemed to her just then, how well one could make out the shapes of things in the night. Or perhaps it was her memory as much as her sight that informed her perception of the room, her familiarity with the objects here, their place and importance in her daughter's cosmos. There were the dendritic silhouettes of the swimming trophies, the stout jars of homemade preserves that her aunt sent every year and that her daughter preferred to collect than open. There was the fat scrapbook with a shelf all its own and there on the old armchair would be the clothes laid out for the day. Except the clothes weren't on the chair—the clothes were tossed to the floor and there instead was her son sleeping under his summer blanket. What on earth was he doing here? Her husband must be responsible. Or had her son wandered in here of his own accord? It was rare that she didn't put him to sleep herself and perhaps, thinking his mother gone, he'd sought his sister, needing a feminine presence. For once he looked comfortable rather than contorted, his body curled neatly between the bulky armrests.

She shuddered to think what might have happened had she gone to her son's room first, rather than her daughter's, and found him missing. What clamor she might have raised, what panic. Her husband leaping from bed, her husband come running. She would have accused him of negligence or worse and all the worst fears would have been confirmed and her daughter would have woken, and her son, they would have been frightened by the tumult and it would be hours if at all before they could be gotten back to sleep. And all the commotion because she would have failed to remember that there are explanations other than trouble to account for life's surprises; that there is serendipity, too, and one might even say good fortune; that for every tale of sudden calamity there are hundreds of unheralded moments like this one, when the son finds comfort from his sister and a bond is formed that outlasts the night.

She could stay in the room with her children, but her son had taken her place in the only chair. It wouldn't do to sit on the floor. No, that wouldn't do at all.

THE SERIAL ENDPOINTING
OF DANIEL WHEAL

The first time Daniel Wheal endpointed was at age twenty-nine, during a picnic with his girlfriend, Charlotte, and her friends at River Park. On the wooden platform between the tennis courts and the dog run, enjoying one of the first days of spring. Unoiled bicycle gears, the tiny cacophony of birds, fellows shouting from the tennis courts with laughter, the river churning past with icy remnants of winter, the creak of sprouting branches as they rubbed against each other in the breeze. They ate pickles and pimento cheese sandwiches while talking about the city's problem with nuisance animals, the best places for a river swim, and fashionable wool accessories, and it was all cordial and enjoyable—except on such a gorgeous day, Daniel grew restless: he hated inertia, didn't believe one should sit still for long. "Let's hit the playground," he said, already on his way. Charlotte and Wyatt joined him; they started at the lumberjack log, where Daniel ran in place without holding on to the rail. Charlotte didn't try, for fear of injuring herself before her next performance; Wyatt tried but when he let go of the rail, he grabbed it again to keep from falling. At the high bar, from a standing position on the ground, Daniel executed a saut de précision in which he landed and balanced on the rail. Then he turned to the climbing wall that connected at the top to various slides; executing a moderately challenging passe muraille, he ran full speed, leapt and pushed off the wall with his left foot, propelling himself high enough to grab hold of the top then swing his feet onto the platform. These were all basic parkour moves—he'd only been trying the sport for a year but with his slender frame (which Charlotte called muscular but undernourished), it came naturally.

Charlotte was impressed and Wyatt, too, although that wasn't always the reaction that Daniel received when he did parkour in public. He'd often been scolded by people who had no personal connection to the building where he was practicing parkour—e.g., a parking deck—but who believed that it was their duty to protect the structure from violation, when what was actually being violated wasn't the parking structure but their own sense of safety and decorum. One woman said to him, "You ought to have better things to do than be a hoodlum, young man." He liked how traceurs talked about parkour as if it were a martial art, emphasizing the rigorous, regimented training, the willful exercise of body and mind to overcome human constraints. But many also believed that parkour, like a martial art, could be used to protect against attack, which didn't appeal to him at all. For example, Elliot Orfall, who practiced "escape routes," imagining himself confronted by hoodlums and using parkour to elude capture in a Hollywoodian chase. That bothered Daniel: he didn't want to walk around the city that he called home looking at every stranger as a potential aggressor; also, since Port Union was relatively safe, imagining that your life was threatened by nameless pursuers was sheer fantasy.

His last attempt at playground parkour was at the swing set; the saddles were ghosted with the outlines of evaporated puddles. Charlotte swung with girlish ungainliness, letting her feet dangle. "You know what is so impressive about your—what do they call it? Parfloor?" She knew it wasn't called parfloor but liked to tease. "It's so shocking when you do it. Calm one minute, next minute you're flying through the air. I mean, you don't look like the kind of guy who can scale a wall like Aquaman."

"You mean Spider-Man?"

"Whatever."

"What kind of guy do I look like?"

"Hmm. That is an interesting question." Swinging, twisting, dangling. "I think," appraising him with her sideways glance, "you look like a sexy bicycle mechanic who probably enjoys comic books too much."

"He looks like a diplomat," said Wyatt. "From one of those northern European countries who carves tiny figurines out of ice and enjoys cruel, meaningless sex."

That got a laugh from Charlotte, one of her breathiest, most delightful laughs, the only laugh that Daniel had ever heard that was actually constituted of the sounds *ha ha ha!*

He started swinging and soon gained good altitude, kicking forward; for an instant, at the apex, the swing chains went slack then jerked taut again on the descent, swinging higher as Charlotte whooped with appreciation. From this height, he could see the river escaping its concrete barriers and rushing into Lake Dominion, inspiring in him the need to swing faster, farther, higher, better—to break free from limitations. Just before the peak he leapt. When he hit the ground, he attempted a roulade to disperse the impact across his back but his left foot landed on a root, tweaking his ankle, sending him sprawling.

"Oh my God!" exclaimed Charlotte. "I'm pretty sure that's not what you meant to do!" She and Wyatt helped him back to the platform. His ankle was throbbing, but he anticipated only a minor strain. The others began a game of Twister as he lay on the platform with his foot elevated on an ice chest. Charlotte ensured that he was comfortable then joined the game on the lawn. He wanted her to stay with him but while she offered sympathy, she didn't have much patience with illness and injury—the slightest impairment unnerved her. Besides, she claimed to be an accomplished Twister player, and as Daniel lay on his back, he tried not to get jealous as she joined her friends on the brightly colored mat, contorting herself over, under, and between the bodies of Wyatt, Jake, and Baldassano.

"Left foot yellow!"

"Oh—excuse-moi—no, I take that back, excuse-toi!"

"I'm pretty sure if I try that, I'll twist an ankle."

"Aw, we miss you, Daniel!"

"You can't share one—guys, you can't share spots."

"Baldassano, I love you but get the fuck off my green!"

The lingering contrails of a passenger jet in the blue sky

above, the laughing nonsense of the tennis players who cared little for form and less for keeping score, the tinkling of ice crystals tumbling on the river, clarinet melodies from tinny speakers, the green fluff of sprouts on the trees, Charlotte's laughter from the grassy field of games: it was all a penumbra of impressions he was trying hard to retain—life is lived in an instant poised on the balls of your feet on the beam.

He dozed.

Then he felt himself grabbed on either side and abruptly lifted.

At first he thought it was a gag from Charlotte's friends, kidnapping him for Twister, so he didn't react. But then opening his eyes he saw two men, one looming on either side wearing surgical masks and Surge's stiff orange jerkins. Shuffling sideways, they laid him on a plank, then lifted the plank intending to carry him off the platform, where a gurney waited to receive him. He sat upright on the plank and looked wildly about. His friends had fled—their crumpled Twister mat was blown in the wind. Not only his friends but everyone else: the crowd that only moments ago had been enjoying a pleasant Sunday afternoon in the park, now all—even Charlotte—had fled Surge.

"What's happening?" he exclaimed, looking back and forth between the two men, who didn't seem surprised by his ability to sit up—nor that he was able to speak.

"They go on twitching for hours," one shrugged.

"Piss himself yet?"

"I hate it when they piss themselves."

"More corpses these days—pissing themselves. Ever notice that?"

"I'm not a corpse," said Daniel. "You can see for yourself!"

"He says he's not a corpse."

"That twitching tongue. Disgusting. Get him out of here before I puke."

Seeing that the opening between the platform rails wasn't wide enough to carry him sideways, they turned so that the bulky officer now had his back to the steps, facing him, shuffling backward. He had looming eyebrows and a soft, pale, rectilinear head like a bar of soap. Both men had an antiseptic quality: the skin of their faces looked bald like a plucked chicken. He had only once encountered Surge at close range—at thirteen, Aunt Marnie took him shopping at the mall then collapsed at the food court. He didn't know what to do. She was lying on the dark-green octagonal tile. Her dress was disheveled, her silk scarf flared, and her eyes were fixed open in an alarmed but courteous expression as if she'd just stepped up to the cashier and realized she'd forgotten her purse.

He sat on the tile and clutched her hand. He heard footsteps.

"Son, you've got to come with me."

He heard the man shift his weight.

"Son, this instant."

"Jim! Jim, they're coming!"

"Go on, Rebecca, I'm right behind." And the man's thumb dug into his shoulder. "She's endpointed, son. Endpointed, I'm telling you!"

"Dammit, Jim, hurry."

"Now, son! You've got to come now!"

He looked in horror at his aunt and saw that her eyes had gone flat and scummy like stagnant water. He smelled something fecal. A flesh fly alighted at her nostril: she was no longer living but a corpse—a filthy, contaminated corpse—but he couldn't abandon her. The man and his wife left him and he felt small and vile and alone on the floor of the empty mall. When Surge arrived minutes later they kicked him with a boot to the gut. He didn't let go of her hand and they grabbed his hair and yanked so hard he was hurled back onto the steps. They hooked her under the armpits and dragged her toward the gurney, her high heels clicking along the gaps in the tile.

On the platform at the park, he demanded to know where Surge was taking him. "He better shut that flapping mouth," said one.

"Before the maggots get in," said the other and stepped backward off the platform, holding the plank level as he reached the ground.

Daniel swung round off the plank, dropped to the platform and in two quick steps, ignoring the weak ankle, side vaulted over the rail. On impact he executed an adequate roulade and then, back on his feet, hardly feeling the pain, he came to a flatbed gardening truck blocking passage between two hedges and he cleared it with a traveling kong vault; on landing he felt a twinge in his ankle but ran on toward the river, where he followed the path along the concrete bank to the pedestrian bridge and there at the height of its arch paused to look back. Surge had given no pursuit—they dealt with corpses and corpses didn't run.

He looked back again for Charlotte, but Charlotte was gone.

The second time Daniel Wheal endpointed was a dozen hours later, in the second-floor bedroom at his row house on Key Street a half block south of Duchess. After fleeing Surge, he had spent all afternoon at home, awaiting a call from Charlotte that never came. She failed to answer his calls or respond to his messages, in which he reassured her that he was not endpointed but alive and well, speculating that the incident was probably caused by a glitch in the software that Surge used to locate corpses. The corpse they were actually looking for was probably hidden nearby. He tried to sound confident but in reality, he wasn't sure. Police shot children; courts convicted innocents; fat-necked councilmen defunded libraries—city services were notoriously defective. Not Surge. Surge didn't make mistakes. EMTs might take an hour but Surge arrived within minutes without exception and without being called. They seemed to be affiliated with no city agency. Shadowy figures, less than human. Now he was finding it difficult to reconcile this prevailing view with his own encounter—they were unspectral, exceedingly corporeal: foul-mouthed, hairless and antiseptic. The Surge of legend would never make a mistake, but as for the two officers at the park—from them a blunder seemed possible.

At home he tried to distract himself with projects from work but found it difficult to concentrate. He kept peering out the curtains for Surge. He kept recalling that repulsive image of Aunt Marnie, the fly exploring her nostrils, crawling into her gaping mouth, roaming the fleshy landscape of her tongue. All she had to do was flinch to dispel the fly; it was her inertia that disturbed him. A corpse was a metacognitive error, a failure of volition. Most humans became corpses because they let themselves go, smoked, drank, ate too much, failed to hydrate, failed to exercise, failed to manage their anxiety and fear. That was Aunt Marnie, addicted to gambling, wasting her wealth on Big Bertha slot machines until, nearly penniless, she begged his parents for help. A corpse was a failure, whereas he possessed an inexorable drive to act, to do, to move.

Late afternoon on Sunday, he again fixed the bathroom faucet—the threads were stripped, so every few weeks after he'd tightened it, it began to leak again. The dripping bothered him, called to mind the water torture of underground dissidents—but he hadn't yet found time to replace the fixture with a new one. While he stir-fried a simple healthy combination of noodles and arugula, he did toe raises on his good ankle while hydrating with water fortified with essential microcarbonates. After dinner he filled the tub, running the water extremely hot; he liked to sink down to his chin, feel the sweat emerging on his forehead. He relaxed by imagining his antagonists dissolving in the steam.

He toweled off, drank one last glass of water, brushed his teeth, and fell into bed.

Minutes later, drifting off to sleep, he heard a rap at his door.

Living only a block from the bars on Duchess, he got his share of drunks knocking on the wrong doors. Generally he didn't answer but it could have been Charlotte, who might miss a dozen phone calls caught up in some adventure, then suddenly realize what she'd been neglecting and rush to make amends. Except through the spyhole he saw not Charlotte but the hulking hairless bodies, the stiff orange jerkins of Surge. One stood aloof, waiting to enter, while his partner returned to the wagon parked in front, with its silent siren and double orange stripe, rear hatch gaping open to receive him. From the back of the wagon, he withdrew a Halligan to break down his door.

In his underwear he ran upstairs to get dressed; as he pulled on his shoes, he heard the Halligan slam into the door, the door splintering as it was pried free from the jamb. They proceeded straight across the foyer then upstairs, knowing exactly where to go. They weren't ignorant louts now; hearing them trudge upstairs with that Halligan in the dark, he was terrified. He kept a baseball bat in the closet for intruders but it seemed inadequate against such assailants. The window was cracked open, allowing the burning-tar smell of skunk to infiltrate the room; the pale-green light from the clock gave off a ghastly glow. He cranked open the window, kicked through the screen, crawled onto the roof above the porch. Below was the Surge wagon, hatch gaping open. The quavering night air was growing cold.

Through the window he saw the dark shapes of Surge enter his room.

"Hey, corpse!" shouted Surge. "Get your maggoty ass in here!"

"You believe this? I gotta go out there and break my neck?"

"Get me a fucking lasso."

Their voices sounded clean, porous and abraded, like volcanic rock. They made no attempt to climb onto the roof but stood looming at the window. The roof above was too high to reach without a running start but he managed by way of a modified passe muraille, shoving off the casement window, to grab hold of the drip edge and pull himself up. He ran west across the adjoining roofs, then came to a six-foot gap separating his row from the next, which he leapt at full speed, catching hold of the opposite roof with a saut de bras and pulling himself up onto his feet. Only now did he look back—neither officer had followed. At the end of the block he dropped onto Lifton. From there it was a block east to Duke, where he headed north.

Once again he had escaped Surge, only it didn't seem he'd escaped—instead he felt the thick pulse of something foul like sewage in his veins. What did it mean to endpoint? You no longer existed. He thought of the vanishing points in paintings, the way the lines receded quietly and geometrically into the distance then disappeared. But where did you go? You weren't supposed to dwell on it. You were meant to understand that the bodies were eliminated, although there was the vague prevailing notion that some essence remained:

their consciousness like water poured through the sluiceholes of the universe.

Charlotte lived east of Duke next to a halfway house for derelicts and drunks, who squatted against the building in the shadows to shit, waking her with their shouts in the middle of the night. Charlotte didn't mind—she believed her neighbors gave her existence a gritty authenticity. She lived at the end of the hall. He stood before her door feeling depleted of strength and usefulness, feeling the hard lean of the floor like the tilt of the world knocked awry. He knocked. He needed shelter. He needed her.

Almost immediately, as if she'd been waiting for him, she called, "Just a minute!" She opened the door then stopped, gasped, tried to slam it shut but he got his foot in. With more force than he intended, he slammed into the door with his shoulder, the door hit Charlotte, she stumbled back, and with an aggression he didn't recognize he grabbed her arms and shook her, shook hard. "What the hell's the matter with you?"

With a flinch, she freed herself from his grip. She wore a thrift-shop dressing gown, like a cross between a smoking jacket and a kimono, deep, inky black with flamboyant embroidery. She pulled the jacket tight and retied the belt. "I'm sorry," she said, and he detected the play of terror on her lips, "I've never had a corpse in my apartment before."

The casement windows had no coverings but you couldn't see outside because of the lamp's bare-bulb glare. The clock ticked, the toilet trickled.

"Look at me," he said. "I'm here, talking to you. I can't be endpointed, can I?"

"You're asking me? What do I know about corpses? Chickens run for miles with their heads cut off!" She leaned against the wall, twisted her arms into a rigid self-embrace; her long fingers gripped the bone. "You smell, Daniel. You smell like I don't know. Polluted river marsh." Reflexively she glanced at her wall display, where, above the stacks of books, she pinned photos of eccentrics from the neighborhood: a woman in a fencing helmet riding a bike, a man in a leather jacket walking stiffly down the street with a FOR SALE sign taped to his chest. He had become one of them, one more freak providing her with urban authenticity. Was that prickle on the skin his flesh rotting from within? "It's weird," she said, "because it's like what happened with my father, when he endpointed and I couldn't get away." And she let out a sputtering laugh that she abruptly restrained. "You men are so narcissistic. You can't endpoint without causing trouble for everyone else."

"Your father endpointed in front of you?"

"We were on his sailboat—windless day so he was having trouble tacking or whatever."

"You never told me."

"He endpoints right in the middle of the lake, no lifeboat so no escape. And my brother couldn't get the boat going either. Of course he endpointed in November, the water was too cold to swim. I was terrified. I'd never seen a corpse before and now I was trapped on a boat with one in the middle of waterworld. His eyes looked like yours—that roadkill quality. The smell was awful. Oh, and there were flies. Where did flies come from? Do they live underwater waiting for a corpse to come floating along? And you know what else? He didn't care. He did this to his children, but he was lying on deck without a care in the world. He was always a bully and that's how he endpointed, bullying me forever because I can't forget his disgusting face. I panicked. We're going to catch some awful disease, we'll never make it home alive! Finally after what must have been hours, Ivan grabbed an oar and shoveled the body off the deck. Here's the worst part—he floated. He kept knocking against the side of the boat. It took Surge I don't know—an hour? Because apparently they're not well equipped to handle boats. On land they quarantined us two weeks and burnt the boat to ash." She laughed bitterly. The bare light bulb flared. The toilet's trickle had a rhythm, there were registers of sound. She dropped onto the futon, her toned dancer's legs tucked precisely inside each other. Her hands were always aware of her legs—caressing her knees, running lightly along her thighs, as if she drew from them some primal, leonine strength. "And now here you are end-pointed just like my father and too much of a bully to leave me alone."

He thought he could detect from himself the faint reek of something rancid. On that futon only yesterday Charlotte had given him oral sex, the breeze from the pedestal fan teasing at her sweaty bangs. Only yesterday he sat on that lumpy futon and she bucked against him, the cool seamless immediacy of her flesh, the tilting pawnshop coffee table, the dimpled petals of the succulents, the shudder of the refrigerator, the relentless exquisite throbbing in his dick like some savage galactic paroxysm and she whispered with increasing urgency as he tried to live, to live, to live—to relish the sensual experience, to transform the moment into eternity.

That was memory. That was past. And Charlotte was past and the past is past. As much as he wanted to relish the experience, he couldn't hold on to the moment, the moments slipped free too quickly, before he could appreciate them the moments ghosted into memory. Time is an endpoint that renders pleasure into a grasping after nostalgia.

The third time he endpointed was lunch the following afternoon, in the nap room at the offices of the Handley Corporation, where he was a junior associate. Leaving Charlotte's apartment, he had feared returning home, so he walked a mile north to the office. He keyed in and stumbled to the nap room, where he might snatch a few hours' rest before the workday began. But the nap room was locked, so he retreated to his desk, where he doodled at various projects, unable to concentrate, waiting in keen anticipation for the arrival of his colleagues.

When they arrived, no one noticed that he didn't belong among the living. At the water cooler, there was talk about yesterday's trade between the RedBirds, Port Union's baseball club, and their archrival. It was reassuring to hear such talk— reassuring to find himself among colleagues who had nothing more pressing to discuss than the blunders of their favorite team—to hear the whir of the copy machine, the burble of the percolator, Ackerman rattling ice in her cup, the cheerful irritation of the HR manager taking issue with Spender's tendency to eat fermented soybeans that bestenched the office. Daniel was just another employee, hunched over his desk, emitting no smells.

"Hey, Wheal, do you have the isometric plan for that bio—whoa, hello, rough weekend, what happened to you?" Charlie Spright, team lead on the Loosen Avenue project. Wild hair, thoughtful spectacles, a fondness for orange.

"Didn't get much sleep last night."

"No kidding," he said and whistled, waiting for Daniel to elaborate.

Daniel didn't elaborate.

Like many Handley employees, Spright wore a watch that started timing when he entered a conversation; it would beep after three and a half minutes, which, according to the latest research, was the most efficient amount of time for casual office conversation. It hadn't beeped yet, so Spright kept talking, revisiting the RedBirds trade. "That Templeton—I'm glad they got rid of him. Sure he's still producing, but too old if you ask me."

"I'm not sure I agree," said Daniel. "With improved physiotherapy methods, he might have three or four more good years."

Spright raised a finger like a teacher about to instruct a witless child—then his watch beeped: time had elapsed.

"Lovely to chat as always, Wheal! See you at the brown-bag—Eveland's giving a presentation on enhanced reuse modalities."

At the water cooler, Daniel did toe raises while waiting for his bottle to fill. He drank copiously. He felt a stiffness in his neck, a creakishness in his limbs. He had a vague idea that he'd been too anxious the last few weeks—too worried about Loosen Avenue. His escalating anxiety had led to excessive sweat, dehydration. Maybe that's what set off Surge's alarms—the percentage of water in his body had fallen below an acceptable threshold. He returned to the cooler and refilled his bottle.

Outside, he took a short walk, dialing the number only when he was well out of earshot of the office.

"Public Treatment Administration, Bryan Grayth."

"Hello, Bryan?"

"Yes?"

"It's Daniel—we met at the pig roast? You had those homemade kale chips and made fun of me for eating too many."

"Yes! Daniel. My wife made those. I brought the tortellini." He waited for Daniel to compliment the tortellini. Daniel didn't remember the tortellini but complimented it anyway. "Old family recipe," said Grayth. "Not many people know I'm Italian, they assume I'm dark skinned because I tan in those booths. Know many Italians?"

"I don't think so," said Daniel.

"See that's the problem. Growing up in Port Union, we

Italians, we don't feel like Port Unitonians. We're outsiders. Then I go study in Florence and discover I'm not Italian either. I'm some kind of I-don't-know-what."

"That's my problem too," Daniel said. "I'm not sure how to classify it. Could be Emergency Operations or it could be Trash."

"Trash has been experiencing problems. Missing pickups in Ashleyville."

"See that's the kind of thing I'm talking about. Errant pickups."

"You want me to connect you to Trash? Becky Abernathy is working hard over there to get to the bottom of things."

"What kinds of services does Trash provide exactly?"

"Landfill, recycling, compost, solid waste."

"Solid waste—that comprises what?"

"No household toxics. That's your pesticides, drain cleaners, pool chemicals."

"Okay, so if a fellow happens to endpoint, would the corpse be solid waste? Or would that be a household toxic?"

"Sorry—what? You said corpse?"

"This weekend I was at the park, having a picnic with friends—"

"Corpse removal is their own department, but they inter-face with Disease Control. Did you come into contact with a corpse?"

"Not exactly."

"So it was proximity? There's a protocol—did you follow the protocol?"

"It's hard to explain. I was lying on a platform at River Park—and it happened again at home—and here is where the miscommunication occurred, because somehow Surge got the idea—it's probably just a software glitch."

"What exactly are you telling me, Daniel?"

"I'm sorry—see it was Surge who—for whatever reason—and I can think of several reasons Surge would get confused—"

"Surge got confused? Surge isn't Trash. Surge doesn't get confused."

"I understand that, but in this case, they got me confused with someone else."

"Like who?"

"Like someone who—well, that's what they would do, they look for corpses, so they find them. There's a flawed incentive structure that could produce false positives."

"Surge thinks you're a corpse? And now you're making phone calls?"

"Maybe I should talk with Becky Abernathy. I thought I should start with you, since I know you, and, to be honest, it's embarrassing."

"Embarrassing? This isn't embarrassing, this is a public health crisis! Where are you? What was your last name again?"

"No—I'm not anywhere—look, you're not listening. It's a glitch, a miscommunication. Because I'm talking to you, obviously, which means—"

"You're spreading contamination!"

"It means I'm not endpointed yet."

"Is that traffic I'm hearing in the background?

"I'm not a corpse, Bryan."

"Is that the sound of children playing nearby? You ought to be surged, not traipsing around a playground talking on the phone!"

"Daniel?"

"Daniel!"

"Daniel, this is a fucking emergency!"

Back in the office it was impossible not to be troubled by his conversation with Bryan Grayth; he was sweating at the temples and his hands shook. He made efforts to control his breathing. He drank more water. He set out in search of William Eveland, one of the principals, ostensibly to hear his opinions on the Loosen Avenue proposal, but in reality, he needed time in the man's company. His favorite of the Handley principals, a mentor, always a supporter of Daniel's work, which he called *disruptive* and *pioneering*. In marathon planning sessions, Eveland never lost patience, speaking with a passionate, gentlemanly solemnity, leaning back comfortably in his chair and making grand, precise gestures. A conversation with Eveland would reassure him of his place in the human circle. But Eveland wasn't in his office and his secretary said he wouldn't return until noon for the brown-bag lunch. This was disturbing news. He stumbled down the hall back to the nap room, and, relieved to find it open, dimmed the lights and fell asleep.

The door banged open, loud voices, two colleagues. Before he'd managed to awaken fully, they grabbed him, yanked him from the lounge, dropped him like a sack of dirt three feet to the floor.

Except it wasn't the floor it was a plank.

And they weren't colleagues they were Surge.

He had told himself that, if Surge came again, he wouldn't cry out in alarm, wouldn't leap and flee. Since they weren't armed, they posed no real danger, meaning he could converse with them, endeavor calmly to find out what was triggering their alarms. Invite them to the pub, learn more about their families. Having befriended them, he would ask if he might examine the devices that they used to locate corpses—discover the name of the software, contact the manufacturer. Perhaps these Surge officers had been given inadequate training—overworked and underpaid.

That is not how it happened.

When his body hit the plank, he opened his eyes, saw Surge, and leapt to his feet. They made an uncertain attempt to take hold of him; he flung his fists at them and broke free. "For Jesus Christ's sake, leave me alone!" his voice cracked and broke like a child's. "I'm alive! Can't you see?"

He should have turned left. He thought he turned left. Left would have taken him past the front desk through the lobby and out the front doors. Instead in his panic he turned right, thinking it was left, and he ran down the hall and burst through what he thought were the lobby doors only to charge into the brown-bag lunch, where Mr. Eveland was standing at the far end of the room before panoramic windows. It was a relief to see him; his face had the bony sheen of polished coral. Seeing Daniel enter so indecorously, Mr. Eveland paused, tilted his head, studied him with bemused interest, as if he were a cat just leapt out of the dryer. "Well, Mr. Wheal, you decided to join us after all. Forgive us, we started without you. I was just explaining to your friends here—" Then he ceased. Looking past Daniel, he was overcome with horror. "Dear God," he whispered, and as his colleagues turned to look, Daniel looked at them, at their aghast faces, small black eyes. They looked from Surge at the double doors then back to Daniel—Daniel Wheal, deprived of sleep, abandoned by love, afflicted in some obscure way by the curse of mortality.

"Please don't worry," said Daniel. "I can explain."

Abruptly his colleagues stood and stumbled out of the room, giving Surge a wide berth. With a pink-spotted handkerchief, Eveland dabbed the sweat at his brow. Like a captain on a sinking ship, he seemed to believe it was his obligation to hold the line until his subordinates had evacuated. Behind him in the panoramic glass, the boughs of elm trees tossed on the wind. "Mr. Eveland," Daniel pleaded, "I need help. They think I've endpointed—could you contact your connections, someone at City Hall? I apologize—it's a glitch, anyone can see that, an embarrassing little glitch that could be rectified with a phone call."

Mr. Eveland inclined his head toward him as if attempting to hear something, some wordless echo, across a great distance. Then he lifted his chin, fixed his expression into a rigid gaze devoid of sympathy. "We do not employ corpses at this firm, Mr. Wheal."

"No sir—I know you don't."

"There are sanitary as well as ethical reasons."

"I'm aware of that, yes sir."

"I'm disappointed in you, Wheal." He coughed, pulled at the cuffs of his sweater. "You have a talent for rigor and whimsy, which could be channeled for gain—but alas your talent has come to an end." And he looked to Surge and said, "Well? What the hell is happening here? If it's a corpse, take it away!"

Daniel didn't wait for Surge to make a move. Shoving past Mr. Eveland, he escaped out the glass door to the balcony overlooking the parkette with its tossing elms, the wooded ravine. From the balcony it was a one-story drop. He leapt from the rail, executing a passable roulade and cutting across the road, dodging traffic then skittering down the slope into the ravine. He found the trail along the creek and kept running northwest. It was cooler here; he heard the *threet* of crickets and, from the unseen bypass, the low grind of a semi shifting gears. He paused to catch his breath, gasping, palms on his knees. A fly alighted on his hand. He had an impulse to swat it away—but he remained still, observing the meticulous activity of its forelegs as it inspected his skin. He thought of the fly inside Aunt Marnie's gaping mouth, how it investigated the dark cavity like an explorer inside a cave, crawling over the stalagmites of her teeth. Having found her mouth suitable, it would call to the rest of the invaders—here, they had found it at last, a place to lay their eggs, a new home. That's what happened when you allowed yourself to fail—your body was colonized by vermin. If he only knew how to live, he would never allow himself to endpoint.

If Surge caught him, they'd haul him away to . . . where? He didn't know. No one knew. No one cared. No one wanted to be troubled with the fate of corpses any more than they wanted to know what happened to raw sewage or the homeless after street expulsions. No one knew the fate of corpses, but you heard disturbing rumors—corpses heaped in stinking piles on secret islands, corpses run through stump grinders. It was no longer possible to believe that Surge's attention was due to some trifling error. He felt his arteries coagulating, the muscles in his back spasming like the last throes of the mortally wounded. He wasn't ready to endpoint yet. He wasn't ready to be bloodied and dismembered. He found a picnic table, clutched his hair and wept.

At dusk he risked a return home, having nowhere else to go. The front porch was cordoned with orange emergency tape, and the front door, which Surge had destroyed the night before, had been removed, replaced with K3 particleboard, bolted into the brick with masonry screws.

THE SERIAL ENDPOINTING OF DANIEL WHEAL

WARNING. THESE PREMISES HEREBY CONTAMI-
NATED. CORPSE INFILTRATION DETECTED. DO
NOT ENTER! BY ORDER OF: PORT UNION DISEASE
CONTROL AUTHORITY

The sliding glass doors were also boarded up, and the first-story windows. Then he heard the sound of plastic blown taut by the wind and discovered that his neighbor had erected a wall ten feet high of two-by-fours and black plastic sheeting. If Daniel's home really was contaminated, this was a laughable barrier, however he didn't laugh but recoiled in dismay. He might break in but he didn't want to defile his own home.

Long into the night, he wandered the city streets. Road bikes hurtled past, small engines straining like some kind of strangled explosion. Women whispered on high black balconies. Stumbling drunk tourists, lost in search of bars. Little gabled Monopoly houses cowered at the feet of monolithic condominiums. Sleeping bodies twitched atop yawning grates. Rusting pay phones clung to brick like locusts under the pale squares of watery lights. A madman with werewolfian hair gibbered and hit himself with a wrench. He passed fleabag alleys, chain-link wonderlands, vistas of blankets and chrome. A man smelling of excrement with a blitzkrieg expression threw his arm round his shoulder and said, "Right now, funk brother, right now." It felt astatic to be out here. It felt obscene. He felt the corpsification of his body intensifying—felt his lungs gone rigid like sacks dusted in concrete. Felt his saliva congealing. Felt his knees creak as if deprived of lubricant. His brain wasn't a bundle of electric impulses but a lump of putrid dough. He had to keep walking lest his body corpsify into a permanent stiff. Down an alley of graffiti he wandered, painted one-car garages, gory and hallucinatory. Blood-red protoplasmic screech owls, severed body parts floating in a green ocean of ooze, bludgeoned skulls, torpedo-nosed German shepherds lunging free from their leashes. The pin-point lights on the masts of the tower cranes, an unfinished building, bone-white concrete vertebrae, St. Amour Home for the Mentally Insane. In front of the Mnobu Community Center, a crowd of a dozen, wearing shiny pants, waving trombones, cheering in a foreign tongue. To be late at night in the city on the street is to hear a thousand secrets and understand none.

He had no wallet, no money. Morning, he found himself on the pedestrian bridge that he'd used to escape Surge, which linked the Haythorne neighborhood to River Park. There he came across an odd gentleman standing with his back to the rail. Dressed like an impresario in a black Regency tailcoat and gold vest, he had attracted a modest gathering. Unlike an impresario, he did not speak, move, or acknowledge the presence of the crowd—though one could detect a quiver of recognition in his lips at the clink of a coin dropped into the hat at his feet. For a moment Daniel could not determine what about the man had drawn attention. Then he noticed the flies, gathering around his nostrils, mouth, the corners of his eyes. They flitted noiselessly about his face and bit him at their leisure, showing no interest in any of the onlookers but preoccupying themselves deliberately with the gentleman like buzzards at a kill. The gentleman made no effort to swat them away nor did he flinch. Though his face was afflicted with welts the size of dimes, his expression was serene and inquisitive, as if the attention of the flies were a riddle he might mull over for hours.

The impression made on Daniel was so powerful that he groaned aloud. A horde of flies influenced by unseen properties, that had singled out the man in the tailcoat for attention. Daniel waited until the crowd dispersed then drew closer. He asked the impresario why the flies were so attracted to him. The impresario turned to face the river, flowing underneath his feet with the vehemence of a mountain flume. "It is one of my—how do you say? Special talents."

"Talent? But it seems more like a curse."

"What is the difference?"

"A talent is a gift—it gives you an advantage. But a curse—a curse destroys you."

The impresario shrugged, causing a minor disturbance among the flies before they settled back into place. "They both come from the same location. They are both communications from God."

Daniel considered this. It was hard to see what God was trying to communicate by way of Surge, yet the idea was not easily dismissed. He asked the impresario whether he had ever seen a corpse before.

"Yes, of course I have seen corpses. We are living among corpses," he said.

Daniel asked whether in the man's opinion he resembled a corpse in any way.

"Are you looking like a corpse?" asked the impresario. "Is that what you are asking?"

The flies alighted among the errant strands of his hair like a flock of crows on winter branches.

"Looking," said Daniel. "Or any other resemblance?"

The impresario gave the question some thought. He studied Daniel, tugging at his sleeves, brushing the dandruff off his shoulder, taking a step back to survey him up and down.

"You are not alive," he said. "But that does not mean you are dead."

"What do you mean?"

"Corpses are not dead. Neither are you."

"How is it that corpses aren't—?" He hesitated, unable to say the word, which had long ago become taboo. Thinking it gave him a cold, writhing feeling in his gut like a fish on a hook.

"If you spend time with them, you see that they are, how do you say? Changelings."

Daniel thought of the changelings he'd read about in the old fairy tales, elfin visitors from the spirit world who exchanged themselves with children. "Corpses trade places with humans?"

"No no no. I mean it, how do you say?"

"Metaphorically?"

"A corpse is a traveler in a parallel realm. You have no life in your eyes but you are on your way to a fantastical place."

"Can you help me?"

"That is not a question you should be asking."

"What should I be asking?"

But at that moment a mother arrived on the bridge with her young son in a RedBirds cap and the impresario resumed his stance of arrogant stiff-backed nonchalance. Such a horde of flies had gathered on one dangling hand that his flesh seemed alive, like percolating fur. "Don't get too close," the mother warned her son as Daniel continued on his way. What was the question, according to the impresario, that he should be asking? Or was the point that he shouldn't be asking any questions at all? That he should be grateful for his condition, which was supposedly some kind of gift, that he should make the most of it? Perhaps he could offer himself to science. Or, having gained some insight into corpseliness, he could write a book—it would be a prophecy, or a weird fable like those macabre children's tales. And yet to do these things, he had to stay clear of Surge. Maybe he could go on provoking Surge then escaping—but he feared he would lose his mind, or his heartbeat, or whatever it was that still gave him power to keep moving in spite of everything.

To act, to do, to move. That was his imperative. It always had been. But it seemed now like a violation of some incontrovertible prerogative. He had always believed there was a clear division between a living body and a corpse—but the impresario disagreed. How could that be? What was the parallel realm to which he was traveling? He wandered the city, indifferent to thirst or hunger, far from home. Eventually he found himself in the Samsal district, near the far north shore of Lake Dominion, an industrial wasteland where an iron foundry and factories had once predominated, spewing filth into the lake. Cement barricades, blasted windows, train tracks gouged into cracked concrete, heaps of debris, brick walls shearing away from hulking sepulchers of industry. Here, he realized, was the old Global Metals factory, which was legendary among parkour enthusiasts; from the roof, supposedly, you could execute a freerunning bomb vault, over a ten-foot gap with double the plunge. It seemed the thing to do—to test himself, see whether his body was failing or if it could still be challenged in meaningful ways.

He kicked the door and it gave way. Sufficient light entered through the windows to illuminate what had once been an enormous lobby, which had the ammoniac smell of guano. The ceiling leached drips of rust water like a cave. On the floor were the silhouettes of primordial puddles; with their clearly delineated outlines, they looked as if they hadn't evaporated but had been instantly vaporized in some sort of explosion. The lobby's showpiece was a long, bi-level concrete ramp that hung suspended by rickety ligaments of rusting steel. The ramp was so unconventional—replacing the typical staircase—so mischievous and theatrical and unexpected, that he laughed out loud. What mad architect had invented such an absurdity? The ramp extended at a gradual incline over forty feet, nearly the length of the lobby, before curving round 180 degrees to reverse course back to the second level. Where had he seen something like it before? My God, he thought, it's an exit ramp. In the pale, fractal light from the filthy windows, it seemed to offer an invitation to climb upward, to cross immemorial boundaries. He stepped onto it, it swayed like a rope bridge spanning a chasm, but he went on, determined to reach the top. As he ascended, the concrete's condition grew worse, potholed where the surface had spalled. Rounding the curve, he felt the structure lurch, he grabbed hold of one of the vertical steel ligaments but the steel sheared free from the ceiling, the ramp collapsed, and he fell.

When he woke, he was lying beneath a mangle of concrete block and rebar. His head throbbed and his vision was afflicted with spots that pulsed and flowed. He could hear the plunking drip of water, accelerated by the collapse. He could shimmy his legs and feel his feet moving free but his right arm was wedged under a great weight.

How long would he have to lie here before someone found him? Traceurs would show up eventually—or squatters who used the building for refuge. Or maybe he'd be trapped here for days as his corpsification became complete. Would that be so terrible? To endpoint was to disappear into oblivion, but what did it mean to die? To die—he saw this now—was to propel yourself with purpose into undiscovered country. This was the invitation offered by the ramp, this was the communication from the gentleman on the bridge. We deny death, we ignore it, we erect barriers to prevent us from pondering its nature. What would it be like to undertake the final journey not with fear but curiosity and wonder? He had been appointed by the powers of the universe to journey into a strange realm.

And so when he heard the sound of car doors opening and shutting, when he saw the pair of stiff orange jerkins enter the lobby from the far door, he wasn't alarmed by Surge's arrival but trembling with anticipation—whether at the prospect of being saved or doomed he couldn't say. He would be the first of the living to journey to the house of the dead.

They wasted no time, proceeding directly to his pile of wreckage. He heard the grind of their boots in the wet grit, smelled their cologne. They had a wet and sticky look like they'd crawled out of a bucket of varnish. Unlike the other crews, they worked silently, picking their way through the debris and lifting chunks of concrete without need to communicate. Within minutes they had dislodged him. His right arm had fallen asleep; as it woke it radiated painfully with tiny detonations. They handled him roughly but not incompetently as they transferred him to the board. Then they lifted the board and swung him round with such abrupt swiftness that it felt like he'd been roped dangling from a helicopter and was being airlifted with dramatic urgency amid chaos and upheaval. Gone were Surge's stumblings and obscenities, replaced with purposefulness and dexterity. It was a comfort to know that he was in the presence of professionals. He nearly started to cry with something like catharsis as they shuffled out of the factory, maneuvering him expertly through the opening. Outside he heard distant traffic, the jurassic hum of jangling machinery. In another moment they would be at the wagon; the hatch was open and waiting. Perhaps concerned that he might flee or just to make sure that he didn't fall, Surge at the far end of the board locked one hand firmly round his ankle. At the wagon they shoved his board headfirst swiftly into the back like a loaf into an oven.

Immediately something was wrong. The hatch was shut and it was dark—he was in some kind of vault—he reached up to feel a ceiling extending the length and width of the compartment. He was afflicted by a spasm of fear, a premonition of dungeons, medieval torture. The car was moving now, swinging out into traffic, propelled swiftly as the driver switched lanes. Surge remained quiet; no chitchat, no radio. The silence felt oppressive, no longer suggestive of efficiency but hostility. There was a smell, too, a powerful miasma—musty and gangrenous. Now as the car veered between lanes something bumped against him in the dark, something bulging and stubborn, and he knew he was sharing the compartment with a corpse. He hit his fist against the ceiling, flimsy plyboard, hit it again, the board rattled in its braces, hit it again, felt the unmoving weight on the board above him and knew that it, too, held a corpse. He shouted to his captors but the only reply was the wagon's sudden leap forward as the driver raced into another lane.

His determination to journey into another realm had come to this: he was hitting, he was kicking, he was clawing, he was groping. He'd never known how much he loved life until now it was being taken away. He hit the board again, it gave at the corner, hit it again, it splintered and his fist broke through. Through the splintered hole, he shoved his hand, which landed on a lank head of hair. That was the last straw. Were those maggots he felt crawling on the scalp? Had he exposed himself to some leprous contagion? He'd been right all along—corpses were corpses, and he had no desire to be one of them. His hand seized on the plyboard's splintered edge, he wrenched it upward, shoved back the board, and sat upright gasping for air.

In the front seat he saw the team was not two but three—the men who had rescued him plus a woman behind the wheel, divided from him by a clear plastic taxicab partition. They were stopped at a red light, waiting in six lanes of traffic. The two men, noting the disturbance, climbed out and proceeded to the back. When they opened the hatch, he retreated as far as possible, cringing in the corner—but then the traffic light changed to green, the driver gunned it, and the car leapt forward, leaving Surge behind. This was difficult to understand in the moment but he thought about it afterward. Surge was robotically incapable of thinking beyond defined boundaries: a signal said he was a corpse, their task was to remove corpses, they would remove him no matter what. The equivalent of the sewage system—an efficient mechanism for the disposal of human waste. The driver likewise had a single purpose: she picked up corpses, drove them to their destination—no matter if she had just lost two members of her team, or that the great wing of the hatch was flapping unaviationally in the back.

Now as the wagon sped down the boulevard, he kicked at the splintered board, sent it flying. That gave him a better look at the corpses who were his companions. What struck him immediately was how undisgusting they were. How serene and dignified. Where was the pestilence? Where were the flies? An older man with red hair in gossamer flares, a round nose, and conspicuous freckles. And lying next to him, a late-middle-aged woman, her eyes were shut and a little sunken, her closed lips had been fixed into a tender, enigmatic smile. Her complexion was pale though her left cheek retained a shy but hopeful blush. Seeing them huddled together at the far end of the compartment gave them the humble quality of a long-wedded couple. Had they died together? He imagined the two of them falling asleep watching TV under a blanket on the sofa, killed in the dark by a leak of lethal gas. They weren't repulsive. And they weren't dead—they were particles of the eternal, like droplets in the water cycle, parts of the superorganism churning through the sequence of transformation and regeneration. The wagon's job was to deliver them on.

When the driver stopped at the next light, Daniel climbed out the back, to the horror of the other motorists. They'd never seen a corpse emerge from a car before. One driver threw his hatchback into reverse, slamming into the truck behind him. Another lunged out the window. Now Daniel truly resembled a corpse, bloodied at the wrist and temple, covered in a pallor of concrete dust. Except he wasn't a corpse. Or rather he was a corpse, we are all corpses, even as we are abundantly alive. The muscles in his back were spasming, only that wasn't evidence of endpoint but energy and strength. He felt his skin tingling with life as if crawling with millions of flies.

He waved to the motorists as he limped past their cars, and he was pleased to see a girl in the back seat with not two but three pigtails wave back.

NOTES

"Spring Leapers" was inspired by a passage from *Hope Against Hope*, Nadezhda Mandelstam's memoir recounting Stalin's persecution of her husband, the poet Osip Mandelstam. Exiled in Voronezh, Mandelstam encountered "sectarians of the kind known as 'jumpers' [who] composed religious ballads of a traditional type about their unsuccessful attempts to leap up to heaven."

The idea for "The Market" came from a passage in *The History* by Herodotus, the ancient Greek historian, in which he claims that a wife auction was practiced annually by the Babylonians: "When the auctioneer had gone through all the best-looking girls, he would put up the ugliest, or one that was crippled, and would sell her off: 'Who will take least money to live with this one?'" Scholar Richard A. McNeal has determined that the Babylonians did no such thing, and while such a finding is interesting, it probably made little difference to Herodotus, who was interested not just in facts but also a people's myths and dreams, no matter how horrible or grotesque.

"The Serial Endpointing of Daniel Wheal" owes a debt to Tim Flannery's review, in the *New York Review of Books*, of

The Superorganism: The Beauty, Elegance, and Strangeness of Insect Societies, by Bert Hölldobler and Edward O. Wilson: "Ant morticians . . . recognize ant corpses purely on the basis of the presence of a product of decomposition called oleic acid. When researchers daub live ants with the acid, they are promptly carried off to the ant cemetery by the undertakers, despite the fact that they are alive and kicking." If it can happen to ants, it can happen to us.

ACKNOWLEDGMENTS

I am grateful to the editors of the publications where several of these stories first appeared in print. Hannah Tinti at *One Story* and Laura Furman at *The O. Henry Prize Stories* ("The Great Fish," originally published as "Conceived"), Ronald Spatz at *Alaska Quarterly Review* ("Spring Leapers"), and Evelyn Somers Rogers at the *Missouri Review* ("Death of the Oarsman," originally published as "Released").

Special thanks to Susan Minot, for finding some merit in these stories, and for bestowing on the collection such an insightful introduction.

Thanks to my agent, Jud Laghi, for his encouragement and expertise, and to the marvelous team at Sarabande Books: Kristen Renee Miller, Joanna Englert, Danika Isdahl, Natalie Wollenzien, Jordan Koluch, and Emma Aprile. Writing is difficult; collaborating with such talented professionals was easy and I'm extremely grateful.

And thanks to the many comrades who read all or portions of this collection and offered guidance when it was badly needed: Alex Ralph, Bridget Robin Pool, Edward Dusinberre, Benjamin Peters, Nicholas Delbanco, Dukes Love, Ben Storey, Chris Love, Elena Delbanco, Chris

Hebert, Dexter Petley, Lizzie Hutton, Josh Ferris, Jeremy Chamberlin, Martin Dusinberre, and Donovan Hohn.

And thank you as well to Peggy McCracken and my fellow summer fellows at the University of Michigan's Institute for the Humanities, who offered thoughtful criticism and intellectual camaraderie.

Also, thank you to my teachers: Celeste Thornton, Fred Allen, Lynn Stowers, Marianne Gingher, Doris Betts, Nicholas Delbanco, Charles Baxter, Ralph Williams, Reginald McKnight, Nancy Reisman, and Eileen Pollack. And to my original writing teacher, my brother, Jack Morse Jr., the first author in the family line, the great adventurer, prankster, and mensch. If such things as creativity and mischief can be taught, I learned them from him.

Thanks to Evelyn, Friday night film enthusiast, robot whisperer, and participant in magical shenanigans, and to Shandy, the napkin bandit: half wolf, half doofus.

Finally, extravagant thanks to Carol Tell: partner, companion, confidante, conceiver, peacekeeper, editor, sanity manager, joke teller, psychic collaborator, provider of metaphysical and material sustenance. "From the onset not great odds, yet she will save and she will bless. . . . For a time—and this fact lifts me up a bit—the universe says yes."

Originally from rural south Georgia, DAVID LAWRENCE MORSE studied in Russia after the collapse of communism, cleaned toilets in Yosemite, and taught English then lived on a rice farm in the foothills of Yamaguchi, Japan, before eventually earning an MFA in fiction at the University of Michigan. He is now the director of the writing program at the Jackson School of Global Affairs at Yale. His work has appeared in the *Washington Post*, *One Story*, *Missouri Review*, *Alaska Quarterly Review*, *The O. Henry Prize Stories*, and elsewhere. His first play, *Quartet*, was performed by the Takács Quartet and the Colorado Shakespeare Festival. For more information about Morse, visit davidlawrencemorse.com.